REAL MEN HOWL

REAL MEN SHIFT

CELIA KYLE

MARINA MADDIX

REAL MEN
ROMANCE

BLURB

Mason's inner wolf will go crazy without her. Lucy thinks he's already crazy. Werewolves aren't real. Right?

Lucy Morgan left Ashtown, Georgia, ten years ago and planned to never return. Unfortunately, life didn't get that memo. She's back and now painful memories follow her everywhere. Until she meets him. Mason Blackwood is over six feet of sinfully gorgeous man who—for some reason—wants her. He also thinks he's a werewolf so... yeah. He's crazypants. But when he wants to have his wicked way with her, his sanity doesn't seem all that important anymore.

Mason isn't sure how much longer he can remain Alpha over the Blackwood pack. Without a mate to balance him, his wolf snatches more control every day. It won't be long before he loses himself to the animal entirely. Then he meets Lucy—a sassy, curvaceous beauty who calms his beast with a smile. One sniff is enough to tell him she's his mate, and nothing will keep them apart.

Not even the pack's deadliest enemy who's determined to kill Lucy before Mason can claim her.

CHAPTER ONE

MASON DOUBTED ANYONE WOULD TAKE HIM UP ON THE offer, but he figured he'd ask anyway. Who knew, maybe there was a wolf in his pack that needed an ass kicking.

He glanced around the clearing, eyes passing over the others. "Who wants to spar with me?"

The glade lay not far from Blackwood pack house, their territory deep in the woods atop a Georgia mountain. Mason and his two younger brothers, Kade and Gavin, had spent many happy—and unhappy—hours in training with the old man. All three of them had practiced controlling their shifts as pups, popping in and out of their wolf form on their father's command. As they'd grown older, they'd learned to fight in the clearing—both as men and beasts. The place held a lot of memories for every member of the Blackwood pack.

Mason yanked his t-shirt over his head and tossed it to his youngest brother, Gavin. Then he bounced from foot to foot, loosening up before his fight. "Okay, who wants to try their hand at besting their alpha?"

The men who'd gathered for early morning training glanced at each other, uncertainty clouding their expressions, and not a one moved. Even Kade and Gavin appeared wary. Yeah, he couldn't blame them for their reaction, but there was no stopping himself either. His wolf howled, the need to hit something riding him hard. The need to release some of his pent-up aggression nearly sending him over the edge. It tore at him, straining his skin and threatening to turn him into a mindless beast.

"Come on, Mason." Kade rolled his eyes. "We're here to train the sentries, not see a display of your magnificence."

Mason ignored Kade's sarcasm and scanned the group of ten or so young wolves. He peeled his lips back, flashing his human-shaped teeth in a feral grin. "What's the problem, ladies?" He held his arms out to his sides. "I promise I won't bite."

Every male in the clearing looked away... except one.

Mason's wolf rumbled in approval, the animal perking up at the idea of unleashing his violence. "Anders, you're up. Although, I'm not sure it'll be a fair fight. In jeans that tight, you'll be lucky to get in one kick before I take you down."

"What I want to know," Anders chuckled and shook his

head. He tugged off his own shirt and padded closer to his alpha, "is why you're looking at my pants."

Mason's smile broadened, and the harsh edge of his bloodlust shaved off with the joke. "Just wondering if they come in men's sizes is all."

Anders narrowed his gaze and crouched into a ready position, fists poised in front of his face.

"Yeah, that's what I thought," Mason snorted and then eased right to circle the man.

He didn't crouch low like Anders. Instead, he stood tall while he countered the other wolf's circles. Anders' shuffled steps brought him close but always just out of reach. Not that Mason was ready to attack.

Truthfully, he hoped Anders would submit before his wolf was challenged. Deep down, he knew Kade was right. He shouldn't be sparring with any of 'em. Train them? Yes. Absolutely. Spar one on one? When need rode him hard and his anger was on a hair trigger? No. It wasn't fair. More than that, it was dangerous in his current mood. Mason had superior strength, speed and wits. Anders was a good sentry, but he stood absolutely no chance of winning. Fuck his chance of learning anything. Yet Mason couldn't force himself to stand down.

Anders lunged and then scurried back. Mason didn't even blink, much less flinch. He'd seen Anders' intent in his eyes a split second before the other wolf tried the bit of misdirection. Mason had seen too much in his life to be fooled by such an obvious feint. Still, his heart pumped fast and hard, and his wolf growled to be set free. They were both ready for a fight—for a *win*—even one as lopsided as this battle would be.

"Mason," Gavin called out to him. "Knock it off, already."

Mason's gaze shot to his brother, eyes narrowed in warning. Anders took advantage of that hint of distraction. Obviously, Anders had thought his alpha was distracted. That maybe he'd gain the upper hand. He was wrong.

Anders leapt forward, his right arm cocked back, and left lowered a hint too much. Leaving himself open, it was easy for Mason to jab the wolf in the nose—the crack of bone signaling he'd broken his sentry's nose. The wolf shook his head, sending blood to splatter on the dirt as he tried to clear his head after the painful punch.

Mason hadn't even put much effort into the strike.

"And that's enough," Kade strode forward until he stood between the men.

Mason's wolf bristled, furious at his brother for stepping between him and his prey. He caught his brother's eye and snarled his displeasure. "Get back and stay back." His gums throbbed, wolf fighting to push his fangs free. "Don't make me tell you again."

Mason ignored his brother's frown. He also ignored the expressions of the other sentries. They'd never seen their alpha so uncontrolled—so on edge—but he couldn't stop himself. Besides, everyone needed to blow off steam occasionally.

"Get up," he snapped at Anders. "You're fine."

Anders sprang to his feet, still wiping the torrent of blood from his nose. The wolf wavered in place, a bit less steady than before, but fight still lingered in his hungry stare. Anders bounced from foot to foot, moving sideways as he and Mason circled each other. Every few seconds, one would push forward and throw a jab, the other avoiding it easily.

"Good," Mason grunted, though he was anything but happy about his opponent's ability to evade him. "You're quick on your feet, but you can't bounce around like a bunny all day."

"Maybe *you* can't," Anders gave Mason a cocky wink. "It's easy when you're young."

If Anders had said that to anyone else, Mason would have laughed. Trash talk was expected while sparring. Hell, it was encouraged. Except this hit Mason in a sensitive spot. Thirty-four wasn't old by anyone's standards—unless the person was an unmated werewolf alpha.

He peeled his upper lip back in a fierce snarl as he glared at Anders. His blood burned hot, too hot. Fury burned in his gut and he'd never wanted anything more than to punch the mouthy little shit across the clearing.

With a growl, Mason swung his arm wide and saw his fuckup in an instant. He'd let Anders get under his skin, dammit. The sentry recognized the opening and took his shot—right into Mason's kidney.

Mason spun away from Anders and pretended the blow hadn't hurt, even though his back burned like a raging fire. "Lucky shot."

Anders grinned, blood staining his teeth pink. "Depends on who you ask."

Anders executed a roundhouse kick, probably hoping to capitalize on his last hit, but Mason was back in the game. He grabbed the man's ankle and gave him a hard shove so that Anders landed on his ass, almost in the same spot as before.

"Who you want to ask?" Mason tried to smile but couldn't hide the falseness. He was far too angry for good-natured ribbing. His wolf strained against his mental leash, scraping and clawing at his human skin. It wanted to turn this spar into a true fight.

In an instant, Anders was up, bouncing around Mason once more. What would it take to make this guy stay down? Didn't he know he was fighting his *alpha?* He had no hope of winning, yet he kept returning for more. Part of Mason admired the sentry's tenacity, but a bigger part of him wanted to rip out Anders' throat and howl his dominance to the sky.

Shaking the thought away, Mason pushed his beast back.

Unfortunately, it didn't want to remain behind the scenes while Mason had all the fun. It wanted to play, too. It wanted to taste blood.

Anders' blood.

Mason lashed out, but Anders bobbed away. The other wolf ducked and weaved, always staying just out of reach. Until he managed to get behind Mason and landed a solid punch to the back of Mason's head.

That one strike had been too much for his wolf. A fine coating of dark fur pushed through Mason's pores to dust his skin. He spun and threw his weight behind a hard uppercut, but only managed to graze the sentry's ear. *Fucker.*

"Dammit!" Mason hissed.

With the clarity only his wolf had, Mason realized Anders was trying to wear him out. The kid knew he would never be able to match Mason's brute strength, and the only way for him to stand a chance was to wear out his opponent. Smart wolf. Solid tactic. It still pissed Mason off something fierce.

His canines dropped through his gums, and it took half his remaining strength to keep his wolf under control. The beast wanted to leap forward, take Anders by the neck, and shake him until he lay limp and bleeding.

This was supposed to be a bit of fun, he reminded himself as much as his wolf.

7

Only the fight felt all too real. As if the wolf shifter challenged him for control of the pack. The moment the thought formed, it refused to be banished, making his blood boil over.

Mason tackled Anders, fury shoving him into action as he threw aside any pretense of play. They fell to the ground together in a tangle of muscled limps, and Mason reveled in the flash of fear in the sentry's eyes. Mason's wolf howled in triumph. It seemed Anders finally understood who was alpha, and who would *remain* alpha.

With the wind knocked out of him, Anders didn't put up much of a fight any longer. He didn't struggle as Mason straddled him and rained down a storm of punches on the other wolf. Blow after blow, he released his pent-up fury on the bleeding man. Yet it wasn't enough to slake his thirst for blood. His wolf howled to be released, to be freed to cause more damage—an idea that intrigued and excited Mason's human half.

Mason let the wolf come forward and just as he started his transformation, strong hands—many of them—hauled him off Anders and threw him to the ground. Before he clambered to his feet, the men in the clearing surrounded Anders—the sentry lying in a bloody heap. The sight of them standing there, protecting their pack mate, drew Mason back to his senses. A switch had flipped, bringing him out of the fetid darkness of bloodlust.

"Shit," he rasped, scrubbing a hand across his scruffy jaw.

Kade and Gavin strode forward and forced Mason to turn in the opposite direction. They hauled him out of the clearing and away from the mess he'd created. No one spoke until they were out of earshot of the others. He glanced back for one last look at Anders, and regret wrapped around him with a strangle hold. At least the wolf was upright now, leaning against his pack mates.

"He'll be fine," Kade gave Mason a shove. His words were probably meant to be soothing, but his younger brother's tone held a surge of anger. "I need you to focus on something else. We just got a call. There's a fire on the north ridge of our territory and it doesn't look like it's going to slow down. Time for you to put on your park ranger uniform and get your ass down there."

"We'll go with you," Gavin added quickly. "I'll send Drew to tend to Anders. Maybe we can keep this quiet."

"Fat chance," Kade said with a humorless laugh.

Mason gripped a handful of his own hair and pulled hard —using that small sting to make him focus. "Don't bother. Everyone knows what's happening. No point in pretending otherwise."

They walked in silence for a moment before Kade spoke, his voice gritty with emotion. His brother's emotional pain teased his nose. "You're losing control."

Mason nodded. His stomach threatened to spill his breakfast on the forest floor, but he pushed it back. He shoved his regret back, too.

"It's coming on fast." Mason's wolf added a growl to his words. "Without a mate…"

Kade picked up the thought. "Without a mate, you'll turn feral. We'll have to kill you so you don't attack the pack. Then the National Ruling Circle will select a new alpha, beta and enforcer to take over Blackwood."

"In other words," Gavin grumbled, "we're fucked."

The agony of guilt at failing his brothers and pack drew a whimper from his wolf. It was the beast's fault as much as his own. Of course, it wasn't as if anyone could force a mating bond. He and his wolf had spent decades trying to find their fated mate, but they'd failed. And that failure would not only bring down him, but his family and pack as well.

Gavin was right. Unless Mason found his mate—and fast —they were all fucked.

CHAPTER TWO

Lucy wove her way down a busy sidewalk in downtown Ashtown, Georgia, darting out of the way of one particularly boisterous child.

"This was a mistake," she mumbled to herself.

No one heard her. No one even noticed her. Still, she would have felt so much better if she'd donned a disguise. Maybe a set of those joke glasses with the giant schnoz and bushy mustache. *Ooh*, if she'd owned a red trench coat, she could have gone full-on Carmen Sandiego. Hell, she would have settled for a baseball cap and a pair of oversized sunglasses. Something, *anything* to feel less conspicuous.

Not that a disguise would have made a bit of difference. After a decade away, she doubted if anyone in Ashtown remembered her. If they did, none of them would ask the questions that really filled their minds. Though Lucy had the answers already prepared.

No, you haven't seen me in a while. Watching your parents brutally killed has a way of making a person want to hit the road.

Then, once the pleasantries of her parents' gruesome deaths had been covered, they could move on to lighter fare. Such as, say, how Lucy's life was crumbling around her.

No, I didn't know you owned a law firm and had three perfect brats. Me? Nope, no kids. No husband or boyfriend either. No job, no friends, no future. Yup, I've got it all figured out.

In reality, Lucy had nothing. Other than the hard lesson she'd learned—once accused of business misdealing, a person was forever damned. Guilty or not. At least, in the corporate world. Any hopes of climbing the corporate ladder were futile and it was hard to wash a resume of that kind of stain.

For some idiotic reason, she'd thought coming home to Ashtown might bring her some comfort. Maybe even a little closure. Except her only memories of the small town centered around family camping trips to the nearby mountains. One trip in particular and one night she'd spent the last ten years trying to forget. For better or worse, she was back. Might as well check out how the town had changed.

Main Street remained the same. Some of the stores were

different, but the potholes in the road were just as large as she recalled. The city council probably didn't want them *too* fixed or it might encourage speeding. It was just like a small town to leave potholes instead of investing in speed bumps.

Across the street, a familiar red awning hung over the place her parents had taken her every week for ice cream. Now the storefront boasted artisanal vegan and gluten-free baked goods. The corner store she and her friends had stopped at for candy after school now displayed a wide variety of essential oils and vape pens in the window. Even the antique stores had fallen prey to the evils of the current trends. Instead of beautiful Victorian furniture, they mostly seemed to offer vintage record players, old box-style cameras, and weird tubs of mustache wax.

Ashtown had turned into hipster heaven! No wonder all the young men with unusually long, perfectly groomed beards and the skinny, young women wearing mismatched shoes and horn-rimmed glasses were looking at her funny. With her full figure crammed into mom jeans and a boring white t-shirt, she must have looked like an alien to them.

Just get the hell out of Dodge, her brain insisted. The temptation to high-tail it back to her car and head for her grandmother's house two hours away was strong, but her need to continue her tour of her old stomping grounds was even stronger. Besides, she wasn't about to be run out of *her* hometown by a bunch of fashion failures.

She just needed a break from all the absurd hipness surrounding her. Up ahead, like a beacon shining through thick fog, a sign she recognized caught her eye. It hadn't changed at all, maybe a little faded, just like Lucy. *Beans*, her favorite little coffee shop when she'd been sixteen-going-on-twenty-six. It sported the same green awning and dozens of flyers for local events plastered the window. Pushing the door open, the same silly chime rang out, announcing her arrival.

The older lady behind the counter stood with her back turned to Lucy while she blended something in an old-fashioned milkshake machine. A beefy guy with flowers braided into his beard and the prettiest pink Hello Kitty roller skates leaned against the counter waiting.

"Extra flaxseed oil, if you can," he said.

The woman bobbed her white cotton candy-topped head and then poured the concoction into the guy's reusable mug before setting it on the counter. Wiping her hands on her apron, she smiled placidly and told him the price.

Lucy nearly choked. Taking into account sales tax, that funky smelling shake had cost the guy fifteen bucks. And he actually appeared pleased about it! As he skated past her toward the door, a piece of straw stuck firmly between his lips, she couldn't help gawking after him for a second.

"Well, look who the cat dragged in," said a raspy voice behind her. "Lucy Morgan, as I live and breathe."

Turning, she greeted her old friend with a smile. "It's good to see you, Miss Violet."

Miss Violet Beauregard had aged as well as her coffee shop. That is to say, barely at all. Maybe a few more wrinkles and a little more white in her hair, but overall, she was the very picture of a sweet Southern lady.

Lucy approached the counter, glancing at the menu board bolted to the wall before refocusing on Vi. She hugged Vi awkwardly across the counter. "And here I thought this was the one place in town that hadn't changed."

Vi shook her head and sighed. "Don't get me started, sugar. But," she shrugged, "if people want cat poop coffee, I'm happy to charge them for it."

Lucy gasped. "That… can't be a thing. Can it?"

Vi nodded toward a couple canoodling in the corner, noses buried in their phones as they sipped from their reusable mugs. "You should ask them. They like to call it kopi luwak, but I just call it cat poop coffee and charge 'em extra for it."

"Um…" Lucy wrinkled her nose and scanned the menu board for something a little less *exotic*.

"Don't worry, honey-pie," Vi reached for a ceramic mug. "I still have regular ol' coffee that'll put hair on your chest, just for locals. It'll cost you a buck, though. Afraid inflation is inflation."

"Sounds perfect," Lucy flashed a grin and dug in her pocket for a couple of bucks—one for the coffee and one for the tip jar.

"You got it, sugar." Vi caught Lucy's gaze as she poured. "So, what do you think of all the changes around here since you left?"

Lucy searched for the right words that would convey her conflicted emotions without sounding rude. "There sure are a lot more vintage record stores than when I was a kid."

"Comic book stores too," Vi added with a wry chuckle. "Antiquing sure has changed, hasn't it? But we've still got the best of the best. Last month, we were voted one of the top ten antiquing destinations in the entire country."

"Wow, that's impressive."

Vi shrugged and held out the steaming cup of black coffee. "Don't get too excited. It was on Hipstermania.com."

Lucy laughed as she took the cup from Vi and tried to hand her some money. Except, the woman waved it away, her hair floating around her head in a cloud as she shook it.

"Consider it a welcome home gift. But don't get any big ideas." Vi narrowed her eyes in a mock-glare, lips twitching. "Next time, you're paying full price."

Lucy grinned. "You drive a hard bargain, Miss Violet."

Rounding the corner, Vi ushered her to a nearby table and sat across from her. "How long are you in town?"

Lucy dropped her gaze to her coffee and took long sip to stall. "I, um... I'm not sure. I just came to check on my parents' house."

"Well, if you get a chance, you really should pop into some of the newer shops. Most of it's not my thing, but you're young and 'with it,' or whatever the kids call it these days."

"I certainly wouldn't say I'm 'with it,' especially considering everything I saw in the windows made me want to throw a brick through them."

Vi laughed so loud she drew the attention of the cat poop-swilling couple. Though not for long because two seconds later, they were back to scanning their phones.

"Well, I can't argue with you there. What no one can argue with is that, ugly kitsch or not, Ashtown hasn't had a boom like this for as far back as I can remember. And my memory is excellent."

"That's great to hear," Lucy was genuinely happy her hometown was doing so well.

"And it's all the doing of Mason Blackwood. You remember him?" Vi gave her a curious glance over her bifocals, a small smile twitching her withered lips.

Lucy frowned. "I don't know Mason, but the name

Blackwood sounds familiar. Kinda reminds me of a couple guys from high school, but they must have been his brothers."

The Blackwoods had been the hot, popular guys and Lucy... had not.

"They're good boys. They've been instrumental in growing Ashtown, but it was Mason's work with the Park Service that really helped. He developed a wonderful hiking trail system through the woods that brought a lot of people to town, and then word spread about all the other wonderful things we offer. Those hipster and outdoorsy types flocked here."

At Lucy's strained smile, Miss Violet gasped and reached for Lucy's hand.

Vi's eyes opened wide at the mention of the woods. "Oh, honey, I didn't mean—"

"No worries." Lucy took another drink.

Awkward silence stretched out between them for a few seconds before Vi cleared her throat and tried again, bless her heart.

"How's Tessa doing? I sure do miss her. You too."

Lucy's shoulders relaxed. "Grandma's still as feisty as ever. I've been staying with her recently, and I tell you, she's still pretty spry. Although I'd be lying if I said I wasn't worried about not being there for her right now."

Vi leveled a mock-glare at her. "I'll have you know your grandmother and I are the same age. We might *look* like dinosaurs, but that doesn't mean we need to be supervised like toddlers."

"Oh, trust me, I know." Lucy released a soft laugh and her smile widened. "It's not her I'm worried about. My friend Ally is staying with her while I'm gone, and God only knows what fresh hell Grandma is putting her through. Ally is a bit of an introvert."

Vi snorted. "I hope your friend has some thick skin."

"If she didn't before, she will by the time I get home. Of course, considering Grandma's taste for prying into business that is very much *not* hers, it's quite likely Ally has already locked herself in the bathroom and is refusing to come out."

Vi laughed heartily, irritating the hipsters in the corner. Actual live conversation must have been more than they'd bargained for when they decided to visit a coffee shop.

"Either that or she's on a flight halfway around the world," Vi quipped.

They sat and chatted—gossiped, actually—for a good ten minutes before new customers wandered in. This time a trio of young women sporting wildly colored hair and carrying hula hoops. Miss Violet glanced at them and sighed quietly.

"Welcome to the asylum," she whispered as she stood.

"Better go help them, but please come back and see me again before you leave town."

Lucy promised she would and then headed outside to resume her walk. Cars whizzed past and she couldn't help thinking the city council's apparent plan to use potholes as speeding deterrents wasn't working out so well.

Just as the thought crossed her mind, the ear-splitting scream of a child in pain filled the air. A flash of grief swelled inside her chest, thoughts of her parents rushing forward. The cry reminded her of her own scream during the attack on them. She'd been paralyzed with terror that night, but she wasn't a clueless teenager now. She hadn't done anything back then, but she sure as hell wasn't going to make that mistake again.

CHAPTER THREE

A LITTLE BOY, NO OLDER THAN SIX LAY ON HIS BACK IN THE street, rocking back and forth as he hugged his skinned knee. His scream of surprise had turned into wails of pain. Lucy glanced around for the tyke's parents but couldn't see anyone near him. What she did see turned her blood cold. A huge SUV bore down on the boy, and even at a distance, she could see the driver staring at his phone instead of the street.

Without thinking, Lucy darted across the road, feet pounding on the asphalt. She bent low and scooped the little boy in her arms, holding him close as she continued her run. Her heartbeat thundered, and adrenaline flooded her brain, urging her body to move faster, push harder. She hadn't even made it to the sidewalk before the SUV sped past. The roar of its engine drowned out all other sounds, and the wind it generated pulled at her hair and buffeted her clothes. As if the massive vehicle fought to capture her, angry it'd missed out on its prey.

Fear plagued her, but it was nothing compared to the boy's full-blown panic. He wriggled in her grip, snarling and scratching her skin. She struggled to hold him carefully as she lowered him toward the ground, unsure if he'd sustained any injuries. It wasn't until he somehow reached her leg with his sharp little teeth that she gave up and let him plop down. The adrenaline coursing through her veins didn't allow her to feel the full depth of the pain, but she knew there'd be hell to pay later.

"Hey, buddy," she carefully turned him by the shoulders to face her, "no need to bite. You're safe. I've got you."

Wild brown eyes collided with hers, utter terror in his expression, and it took a minute for her words to reach him. His expression softened and calmed, his tiny shoulders slouching, and then tears filled those soulful eyes. His lower lip wobbled, chin quivering. *No.* Not a crying kid. Anything but a crying kid. What the hell was she supposed to do with him?

"I'm sorry," he sniffled. "I didn't mean to." He hiccupped and then launched into a long rambling explanation. "I know I shouldn't have. I know it's forbidden. But the kitty was in the road and the big car was coming and I needed to save her and I know pups shouldn't care about kitties but she was so cute and fat—"

His babbling continued, only silenced by a feminine

shout. A beautiful young woman ran to them and kneeled before the boy, checking out his scuffed knee.

"Charlie, sweetheart, what happ—"

The woman stopped talking when she caught sight of Lucy's bloodstained jeans and the pale skin beneath the tears in the fabric. Her eyes widened and she paled at the perfect circle of tiny punctures. Lucy had barely registered the injury, though now that she looked at bite, she wondered how little Charlie managed to chomp deep enough to draw such a steady stream of dark blood.

"Oh my God," the woman breathed, her frightened eyes flicking between Lucy and the still-sobbing child. "Charlie, what did you do?"

Charlie hiccupped and launched himself into his mother's arms, burying his face in her neck. Lucy's heart ached for the little guy and Lucy gave the mom a reassuring smile.

"It's okay. Just a flesh wound, as Monty Python would say. See?" She wiped away the blood, but it was quickly replaced by more.

She frowned, staring at the wound. Strange, it should have slowed down. That was also the moment she realized pain thrummed through her to the beat of her heart. The rush of adrenaline must have numbed her to the pain and it now gradually came forward. Still, it was a bite from a six-year-old, not some massive, feral animal. It wasn't as if the kid had rabies, or something. She'd be fine.

Except the woman had other ideas. "Robert!" the woman shouted, desperately looking over Charlie's head for someone. "Robert! Hurry!"

A tall, handsome man sprinted around the corner toward them. Without so much as a "How dee do," he kneeled to examine her wound.

"What the hell happened, Bonnie?" he asked. He sounded upset, but not angry, exactly. More… frightened.

"I'm fine, really," Lucy insisted. She bent and lowered her voice, speaking directly to the newcomer. "Charlie was just scared. That SUV almost hit him and then a strange woman grabbed him. I know he didn't do it on purpose. It happens." She shrugged, pretending not to feel the rising agony. "Don't worry. I'm not going to sue or anything."

Robert and his wife exchanged dark glances, speaking that strange silent language only couples who've been together for ages understand. Bonnie stood, still holding Charlie in a fierce hug, and stepped back. Robert turned back to Lucy and tried to smile, but it came across like a grimace.

"Miss, would you please allow us to get you treated?"

Lucy snorted. "Treated? I'm sure it'll be fine. I just need a Band-Aid. I swear I'm—"

She broke off when she stood and lost her balance, clutching at her new pal Robert to catch herself before she went ass-over-teakettle into oncoming traffic. Without a word—or her permission—Robert swept her into his arms and headed down a side street. Lucy wanted to object, wanted to feel outraged that some stranger had taken such liberties, but her head was still spinning from standing too fast. Bonnie and Charlie scurried along after them until Robert pushed through a glass door.

Robert gently set her in a chair and then went to the reception desk and whispered with the nurse, their voices too low for her to hear. She relaxed into the seat, and now that she was sitting, her head began to clear. The place didn't smell the greatest, but it had that "doctor's office" feel. She took a look around the space, inspecting her new surroundings, and it didn't take her long to figure out that this place was... different. Instead of dreamy images of clouds with inspiring quotes on them, the frames on the walls featured photos of cute kittens and puppies playing together. Another featured a dog gazing up at its owner in the sunset. There was one that showed a lizard stretched out on a rock in the middle of the desert.

Then the glass door opened, and a woman walked in with a rabbit in a cage.

Dear Lord, she wasn't in a doctor's office. She was at the vet's!

Bonnie took the seat next to her, Charlie still cradled in her arms. She faced straight ahead, but Lucy sensed the woman watched her with her peripheral vision. Probably waiting for the inevitable reaction to being taken to a vet's office.

"This is really nice of you guys," Lucy finally said, standing more slowly, "and I appreciate your wanting to make sure I get treated." She made sure she added the right amount of Southern appreciation. "But I think I'll go to my own doctor when I get home."

"Please let Dr. Cooper take a look," Bonnie pleaded, eyes wide with something akin to panic mixed with horror.

The fear in Bonnie's eyes gave Lucy pause, and she tipped her head to the side, brows scrunched. Charlie's mom was genuinely worried about the bite he'd given Lucy. Maybe the kid had some weird kind of disease? One only a vet could treat? Unlikely, but still, *something* was off.

A tall, handsome man in his mid-thirties, with neatly trimmed brown hair and mysterious grey eyes, strode from the back. A long white lab coat billowed behind him as he moved, and it didn't take Lucy long to deduce he must be the amazing Dr. Cooper. He kneeled in front of them, Robert hovering at his back and chewing frantically on a thumbnail.

"Drew," Bonnie's breath whooshed from her lungs and she sounded more relieved than seemed reasonable. The town really *had* changed a lot. Then she leaned in and spoke so quietly Lucy barely heard her. "Charlie bit her."

Charlie whimpered again and kept his face hidden, buried against his mother's neck. Dr. Cooper, on the other hand, turned as white as Lucy's shirt. Well, as white as it *used* to be. After her adventure, it was more of a grimy grey with streaks of black and splotches of dark red.

"Got it," Dr. Cooper's tone was tense and clipped. "If you'll come with me, Miss…?"

He stood and held out a hand to her. Lucy still couldn't believe she was going to allow a veterinarian to check out her injury. Then again, she'd been bitten by a kid pretending to be a puppy so it kinda made sense? Sighing heavily, she took his hand and allowed him to help her stand.

"Morgan," she answered. "Lucy Morgan."

Dr. Cooper flashed her a megawatt smile and Lucy wondered what kind of insurance she'd need to keep Dr. McHottie as her doctor.

CHAPTER FOUR

THANKS TO THE SMOKE FROM THE FIRE, THE EVENING'S sunset lit up the sky over the mountain with a stunning array of reds. Mason tried to forget about everything that had happened that day, just for a moment, as his government-issued Jeep Cherokee bounced over the rutted road that led to the pack house.

Except, as much as he tried, he couldn't stop those whirling thoughts from intruding. And they weren't pretty. They bounced around as much as his ancient green Cherokee. The topics ranged from how much longer he had before he went fully feral, to how Anders fared after their spar-turned-attack, and then, to who'd set the damned forest fire and why. Of course, he didn't have answers to any of the questions, which only pissed off him *and* his wolf.

Acrid smoke clung to him like shit on sheep, but the

underlying scent bothered him most—gas. It hadn't been an accidental fire started by some negligent camper. Someone had set the fire deliberately, and it had taken a team of twenty firefighters—mostly members of his pack —to contain the blaze. As angry as he was that someone had purposefully put his men's lives at risk, the culprit's identity made him even angrier. That made anger edge toward rage.

The minute he'd reached the epicenter of the fire, his wolf had dug through the scents, past the smoke and gas, to find the unmistakable aroma of wolf. A wolf that didn't belong to him. What fueled his beast's fury the most was that this strange wolf wasn't much of a stranger. Something about the scent tickled a faint memory, but he'd been too busy dousing the flames—and worrying about going feral—to give it the attention it deserved. The Jeep thumped into a particularly deep pothole, jolting Mason from his thoughts and damned near out of his seat.

"Shit." He wiped the back of his hand across his brow, only to find it dirtier than before. "Double shit."

He pulled up to the pack house right at the gloaming of dusk, and he spotted someone sitting on the front porch. The figure raised a hand in greeting and then stood, obviously waiting for him. Mason sighed. All he'd wanted was a shower, half of a cow, and bed. That didn't look like it'd happen anytime soon.

"Great," he grumbled, throwing the truck in park and

bracing himself for whatever fresh trouble was brewing in the Blackwood pack. An alpha's job was never done.

"Evening, Mason."

Of course, it was Drew Cooper, the pack's healer and Ashtown's vet. The poor guy avoided crowds at all costs, even to the point of not stepping foot in his own waiting room if too many patients were out there. And he'd sought out Mason. His shitty day just got shittier.

When Drew stepped closer to shake his alpha's hand, Mason held up his soot-blackened palms and grimaced.

"Trust me, that wouldn't turn out well." He headed toward the back of the house. "I better wash some of this off or Ida will hand me my ass on a silver platter."

He trudged to the water spigot out back, Drew following at a respectful distance. Mason wondered if he should have called for Kade and Gavin first. Just to make sure they didn't have a repeat of the incident with Anders. Then again, he barely had the energy to walk, let alone get into another violent tangle.

"How's Anders?" Mason turned on the water and held the hose over his head. Even in the gathering darkness, he could see the water turn black from all the soot and ash.

"Fine. A few bruises, a good bit of his pride. He's already back on duty."

If Mason hadn't lost control, he might have chuckled at the sentry's wounded pride. Anders didn't have anything to be ashamed of. Mason did. Scrubbing his face harder than was absolutely necessary, he hoped some of that shame would wash off with the soot. He tossed the hose to the ground and turned off the water before facing Drew.

"If you aren't here about Anders, what brought you out?"

Drew's face folded into one of his patented frowns of concern. Mason had learned to heed Drew's frowns because they usually meant something had gone wrong. Mason didn't have the patience for the healer to hem and haw.

"Go on and spit it out."

He took a step closer to get out of the puddle of mucky water he'd created and then…

Mason froze in place, his lungs filled with a delicious scent that called his wolf forward with a single bound. It leapt to the front of his mind, analyzing the scent, and his entire world tilted on its axis. The sharp bite of fire and smoke and the strange wolf no longer consumed him. Instead, the stench was replaced by Drew's familiar flavors tinged with something else. Something that set his heart racing and knees weak.

It was floral yet fruity, sweet with a hint of tang that he could almost taste. His mouth watered, and his wolf howled while his body yearned to be coated in the scent.

His mate.

Mason didn't know who she was, but that taunting scent

was all over Drew. Not just her natural flavors, but the coppery tang of her blood, too. She was injured?

His body moved of its own volition and Mason launched himself at the pack healer, knocking Drew flat on his back. He had the wolf pinned before the guy knew what hit him and his fangs descended, bared in a clear threat. His mate was injured and the man blinking up at him had her blood on him!

Flashing his teeth with a growled warning, Mason glared at Drew. His eyes latched on to the quickly pulsing vein in his quarry's throat, and bloodlust threatened to overtake his control. Drew seemed to sense the danger as well. He froze and dropped his gaze away from his alpha's furious scowl —a sign of submission that appeased his wolf—slightly.

"Where is she?" Mason's hoarse voice rasped from his partially shifted throat.

Drew's eyes snapped up to meet his, widened in surprise. "Mason, listen—"

"You have one minute," Mason released Drew's arms but retained his dominant position. He could only control himself for one minute more and then he'd be lost to the bloodlust. Besides, if he needed to kill the man, he didn't want to have to chase him all over God's creation.

"Her name is Lucy Morgan," Drew fired off the words. "The Tiptons brought her to my office today. She was injured."

Joy at hearing his mate's name for the first time mixed with fear for her safety. Rage and fear built inside him to the point he couldn't tell one from the other. "Why? How?"

Drew outlined the day's events, from Lucy saving Charlie's life, to the accidental bite he'd given her, to Drew doing his best to treat her. The healer took a deep breath and glanced pointedly at Mason's hands. Hands that had somehow latched on to Drew's shoulders and inched inward toward his throat. All on their own.

"I'll take you to her if you'll let me go."

"He's going to let you go regardless," a voice called out from behind Mason.

He spun to find Kade closing in on them. Mason released Drew and jumped to his feet before his brother could humiliate him by dragging him off the poor, defenseless healer.

"Mason, what the hell is going—"

Mason held up a hand to silence Kade. He may have been out of line—common occurrence lately—but he was still the alpha of the Blackwood pack. They could play the "what else has the alpha fucked up?" game behind closed doors.

"How bad is it?" Mason refocused on the healer.

Drew shook his head. "I'd hoped it'd be no more than a

scratch but when I cleaned her wound... Charlie bit her, Mason."

Blood drained from Mason's face and he staggered backward, fully aware of what those three words meant. For her. For him.

"Who are we talking about?" Kade spoke when Mason couldn't.

He couldn't focus enough to answer his brother. His mind was too busy trying to figure out a solution to the problem in front of him. Drew paused, waited for him to say the words, and then finally did the honors himself.

"It appears a woman I treated today is Mason's mate." Drew sighed and ran a hand through his short hair. "Which, obviously means Charlie isn't. Since she's human—"

"Oh shit," Kade whispered. "What's going to happen?"

"Wait. *What?*" Mason snapped, finally coming back to the conversation.

"I thought..." Drew started, his eyes darting nervously between the Blackwood brothers. "I thought you would have known. From her scent."

As soon as the words were out, Mason realized he *had* known. There'd been a soft, almost buttery hint to Lucy's flavors—a telltale sign of her humanity—but he'd been so overwhelmed by the discovery of his mate, he hadn't put it all together.

"We can turn humans. I don't understand why this is such a big deal?"

"Because I'm her mate. If *I'd* given her the mating bite," Mason said in a monotone voice to mask his true emotions, "it would have triggered her transformation from human to wolf."

Kade's confused gaze bounced between Mason and Drew. "But since Charlie bit her…"

Mason didn't have the stomach to answer.

"Well," Drew started cautiously, "she could become very ill. *Very* ill."

"Good God, stop pussyfooting around," Kade growled.

Drew clenched his jaw before spitting it out. "She could die. I came to tell Mason about the breach of our laws, but now that I know she's destined to become a wolf's mate— an *alpha's* mate… I can't be sure how Charlie's bite will affect her."

All Mason heard was "*She could die.*"

He'd waited for so long to find his mate, only to have her snatched away by a cruel twist of fate. No! Not on his watch. He wouldn't allow it.

"Where is she?" This time Mason's tone was calmer, though he was anything *but* calm on the inside.

"I took her to her parents' house." Drew handed Mason a slip of paper with an address scribbled on it.

The healer had come prepared. Mason slapped Drew on the back in a gesture of gratitude. He was a good man and didn't deserve to be treated so roughly—but no one stood between an alpha and his mate.

"Hey, why wasn't I invited to the party?" Gavin strolled up to the trio grinning, but his smile fell away when he got close enough to see the grim expressions on the rest of their faces. Then he caught the varying emotions clouding the air.

"Go find your five best sentries," Mason instructed as he swept past them all and headed for his Jeep.

"For what?" Gavin asked as he jogged to keep up.

"To protect their alpha's mate."

Mason heard Gavin stumble. "We have an alpha mate?"

"Yes," Mason barked. "She just doesn't know it yet."

CHAPTER FIVE

Driving down the street she'd grown up on had been tough. Pulling into the driveway of the house she'd grown up *in* had been almost unbearable.

None of it compared to the gut-wrenching despair of walking through her childhood home.

The cleaning crew she'd hired before driving to Ashtown —along with the gardener and caretaker she had on retainer—saw to everything inside and out. Not a speck of dust or hint of a cobweb lingered. After ten long years, the little house on Maple Street looked exactly as it had the day she'd left.

Maybe if sheets covered her mom's favorite overstuffed chair and her dad's golf clubs, she wouldn't have felt their absence so keenly. She limped around from room to room, touching all the knickknacks and doodads that made a house a home. So familiar. She couldn't shake the feeling they might walk through the door any second, claiming they'd forgotten their car keys. They'd kiss her on the forehead and rush back out, late for work.

Except, that was a silly, childish fantasy. The place on Maple was a mausoleum. In fact, her parents' ashes sat proudly on the fireplace mantle, a bold reminder Lucy would never see them again.

Swiping the wetness from her cheeks, she sniffed and hobbled toward the kitchen, wondering why she hadn't sold the place years ago. Though deep in her heart, she knew the answer. Nothing could compel her to part with the last vestiges of her life before it all went to shit.

Not for the first time, she sent a silent prayer of gratitude to the Park Service. If it hadn't been for the fund they'd set up to pay for her schooling and associated costs, she never would have been able to afford to keep the house. Her parents had paid off the house long before their deaths, and their life insurance had paid the salary of a very conscientious caretaker. After school, she'd lived off what she earned from her job as an accountant.

Now that she was out of a job though...

NOPE, SHE WASN'T GOING TO THINK ABOUT HER EX-JOB. SHE wouldn't think about *that* kettle of fish for the moment. She'd deal with the fallout from that bullshit later. Right now, she was hungry, hurting, and bone-tired.

Glancing at her light grey sweats, Lucy spied a spot of blood peeking through the fabric covering her thigh. The very cute Dr. Cooper had cleaned the bite and bandaged her up driving her back to her parents' house. His attentiveness was sweet but bordered on bizarre. It was just a nip from a little kid, but they'd all acted as if Charlie carried rabies or something.

Regardless, she'd already decided to call a real doctor in the morning, just to double check Drew's work… and maybe start her on some antibiotics. The area around the bite ached and felt warm to the touch, the wound beginning to swell.

"Wouldn't it just be perfect if he *did* have rabies?" she muttered to the still air.

Two bags of groceries sat on the counter, exactly where she'd left them before touring the house. She'd still felt pretty good at the grocery store and had vowed not to stray from her normal diet too much. She'd spent all her life fighting a losing battle against her curves, and she hadn't wanted to slip up just because her life was in shambles.

Vegetables, salads and non-fat everything filled the bags. As she packed it all into the fridge, she regretted her decision to stick to her healthy eating plan. Right then, none of it appealed to her in the slightest. The very idea of choking down a spinach salad filled her with such hatefire she was almost surprised she hadn't spontaneously combusted.

Spinach, the devil's tool.

Luckily, the caretaker had stocked the freezer with tastier, more fattening fare—mostly in the form of frozen dinners —but she spied a tub of her favorite chocolate-peanut butter ice cream tucked in the back. Pulling out a lasagna, she dropped it on the counter with a *thunk* and set the oven to preheat.

Sighing, she leaned back against the counter to wait. Her gaze slid across everything that reminded her of her mom, finally landing on the archway that led into the kitchen. In a daze, she drifted over to it and kneeled down, her fingers lightly grazing a series of marks etched into the doorframe. Her mother's writing noted an age next to each carved line, transporting Lucy back in time.

She'd always groaned when her mom wanted to commemorate how much she'd grown, but deep down she'd loved her mother's excitement. Tears burned her eyes and no amount of sniffing would hold them back. She rested her head against the marks and fought for breath as tears pushed at her. They filled her eyes and spilled down her cheeks, sobs bursting past her lips while she trembled until she had nothing left.

Pain shot up her leg as she stood, but she pushed past the ache and shuffled down the hallway, searching for more memories. She first came to an oblong dent and ghosted her fingers across the indentation. Boy, her parents had been mad when they'd seen the evidence of Lucy's practicing her softball swing inside the house. Though later that year, they'd cheered the loudest from the stands when her team had clenched the finals.

She was torturing herself by seeking out these reminders of her parents, but she couldn't stop. She eyed the stairs, knowing the rooms up there would only bring her more suffering. Hell, even the sound of the tenth stair creaking, as it always did, would probably send her into echoing sobs.

There was a sweet nostalgia drifting through her too— mixing with the dark turmoil. She'd left the house shortly after her parents' memorial never to return, leaving these memories fresh and raw. Though she sensed that the longer she remained in the house, those memories would ease to bittersweet. Perhaps one day they may become simply sweet...

For now, she'd sleep on the couch downstairs. At least for the first night. Besides, she wasn't sure she could make it up the stairs with her leg.

A heavy knock echoed through the house, the front door jarring in its frame, and she nearly jumped out of her skin. She jolted, and a tiny bolt of pain attacked her with the movement. The silence had settled on her like a heavy blanket, so she assumed any sound would have startled her, but this had been no little knock. Taking small, slow steps, she padded to the entryway. Which apparently wasn't fast enough for her mysterious visitor since he decided to bang on the door *again*, the old wood creaking beneath his strength.

"Cool your jets, asshole," Lucy mumbled as she peeked through the peephole.

Oh, damn.

The man on her front porch stood almost as tall as the door itself. She actually had to stoop a bit to see his face. Not that she minded her initial view—muscled chest and tight black t-shirt that accentuated all that muscle-y goodness. But that face...

He looked vaguely familiar, but she couldn't quite place him. Regardless, her breath caught in her chest at his chiseled jaw, covered with two days' worth of stubble. Just enough to make a girl swoon. She caught a glimpse of his eyes and she nearly *did* swoon then. Her parents had taken her on a cruise to Bermuda once and this man's eyes matched the color of the Caribbean Sea perfectly. A lock of black hair swooped down across his brow in a perfect imitation of young Johnny Depp, though he clearly wasn't trying to be someone he wasn't. When he lifted his fist to pound on the door again—his bicep bulging nicely— Lucy's senses returned.

Wrenching the door open, she glared up at him. "Would you mind *not* breaking my door down?"

The devastatingly hot dude on her doorstep glared right back at her. She had no idea what kind of beef he might have with her, but she wasn't about to be glared at without giving as good as she got. Instead of his narrow-eyed stare remaining on hers, his attention drifted down her body.

His focus paused on her cleavage before moving on to her sweats-covered hips, and all the way down to her pretty pink toenails. The return trip was even slower and something about the way he stared made her think of a wild predator—hungry and fierce.

Lucy cleared her throat and arched an eyebrow. "Well?"

He jerked back a little, almost as if she'd just insulted him. Then a veil dropped across his stormy eyes. "I'm Mason Blackwood."

Lucy waited for him to explain why he'd almost knocked her door off its hinges, but he didn't say anything else. He simply looked down at her expectantly, as if she was supposed to know who the hell he was and why she should care. The name sounded familiar...

"*Okay*... What can I do for you?"

"What happened to your leg?" His gaze flicked to the bloody spot that had grown since she'd last looked.

Dammit! It was just her luck to be caught in bloody sweatpants when a sizzling hot dude dropped by for a chat. Still, his demanding tone set her teeth on edge.

"How is that any of your business?" She crossed her arms over her chest.

His jaw worked as she waited. Tension radiated off him in waves and infected her, but he didn't reply.

"I know gossip travels fast in a small town," she huffed,

"but usually folks talk *behind* your back. They don't huff and puff and try to blow your house down."

The guy's lips twitched and he tightened his mouth, suppressing a smile at her sarcasm. That would have been a first. Most men were turned off by her "keepin' it real" attitude. He opened his mouth to speak, but a loud buzz from the kitchen interrupted him.

"What was that?" he looked past her into the house, his body seeming to grow before her eyes.

What the everloving fuck?

"Not that it's any of your business, Mr. Nosy Parker, but that was my oven telling me it's time to pop my frozen lasagna in."

Mason wrinkled his nose in a way that should have insulted her, but it only made her smile over his cuteness.

"You're not eating that crap for dinner."

The fuck?

Lucy stood there, completely gobsmacked. The guilt she already felt for ignoring her diet increased tenfold and fueled her outrage that some random hottie was judging her dining choices.

"*Excuse me?*" she finally managed to pushed through gritted teeth.

Mason backpedaled like a champ, his tone softening right

44

along with his expression, which of course had Lucy melting into a gooey puddle.

Hotties made her weak. What could she say?

"I only meant that you're injured. You need more protein to help your body heal."

Gripping the doorjamb until her knuckles went white, Lucy did her best to maintain her composure in the face of his scorching hotness. His oddly *sensitive* hotness. She had no idea why the guy gave a rat's ass about her, but his attention sent her body into a tizzy.

"I'm fine." She heard the quaver in her voice and winced at the display of weakness. "I'm perfectly happy with my dinner plans, thank you very much. Now if there's nothing else…"

She said it as if she needed reminding. A little childish, but it was empowering to put the hottie in his place.

"Mason."

"*Right.* Mason. Anyway, thanks for your concern. Bye." She said goodbye while her body simply wanted to say *hello, come to momma.*

Lucy's body screamed for her to throw herself into his arms and cover his body with kisses. Unfortunately— fortunately?—the pain in her leg distracted her enough to keep her sanity in place.

As she slowly closed the door in Mason's shocked face, it

occurred to her he'd never given an explanation for his visit, but she'd committed herself to getting rid of him. Besides, if she had to look into those sea foam green eyes for one more second, her resolve would drain away and she'd happily become his sex slave.

That was the last thing she needed.

When the door clicked shut, Lucy closed her eyes and leaned against the frame, listening to his footsteps as he stomped off her porch. She tried to will her heart to slow, but it defied her. Her breathing defied her as well.

Pushing off with her good leg, Lucy prayed that by morning, the crazy day she'd just experienced would feel like a distant memory. Yeah, not happening. She was pretty sure she could look forward to a fantasy-filled night starring the one and only Mason Blackwood. *Yum.*

CHAPTER SIX

M ASON STARED AT THE DOOR. T HE *CLOSED* DOOR.

Closed.

In his face.

By his *mate.*

He waited a beat, half-expecting her to fling it wide and throw that luscious body of hers into his arms. He'd been utterly dazzled by her beauty and couldn't wait to lay eyes —and much more—on her again. Soon.

Her blonde hair was cut into a stylish shaggy bob that somehow accentuated her full lips. He liked that she hadn't been wearing a lot of makeup. Nothing but the thin layer of gloss on her lips that had made him harden in an instant. The oversized sweats she wore did nothing to hide her perky breasts, trim waist and well-rounded hips. As he recalled how they'd stretched against the soft material, Mason imagined holding onto those hips as he slammed into her over and over. Not stopping until she exploded, and he claimed her as his mate.

Perfect. Now his dick was hard as nails.

It didn't help that her resistance turned him on even more than her beauty. No woman had ever denied him. Most pursued him relentlessly, willing to bow to his every whim. If he'd been a different kind of man, he could have easily taken advantage of those ladies. Instead, he'd treated his lovers with the respect they'd deserved.

Funny that when he'd finally found his mate, she'd all but rejected him. Not funny "ha-ha." More like funny "fuck that." Still, he admired her dignity and self-confidence. An alpha mate needed to be feisty. An alpha mate needed to be willing to stand up to him.

With a frustrated huff, Mason spun on his heel and stomped down the steps, doing his best to ignore the wolfish chuckles coming from the shrubs on either side of the porch. At the bottom step, he paused and gave a low warning growl to the sentries he'd brought along.

"Something funny?" He kept his voice low, not wanting Lucy thinking he was truly unbalanced.

Despite the ass kicking Mason had given Anders that morning, the man and his partner, Quinn, only laughed harder.

"Laugh it up, Tweedle-Dumb and Dumber," Mason growled. "We'll see who's laughing in the morning when I spar with both of you at once. I'll be kicking your asses. Again."

Anders stopped laughing first, and then they both groaned and fell silent.

"Quinn, watch the front. Anders, the back. I'll be back in fifteen."

Fourteen minutes later, Mason was back on Lucy's porch and staring at her door while he tried to figure out his next move. A human male would knock politely and wait until she invited him inside. He didn't need his werewolf instincts to know she'd never welcome him. She'd slam the door in his face again and that assumed she opened it in the first place.

His wolf howled at him to break that door down and hunt her through the house. Nothing should stand in the way of an alpha and his mate. Ever. His happy ass should be by Lucy's side, not standing out on the porch like a dog begging be let in from the cold.

Mason huffed. He already knew his mate well enough to know she wouldn't appreciate him bashing her door down. He decided on settling for a happy medium. He grabbed the doorknob and turned. Hard. Too hard, as he discovered when the knob twisted off in his hand.

Oops. I guess it's open.

With an unconcerned shrug, he dropped the twisted bit of metal on the porch and eased the door open. Her scent hit him like a sledgehammer, soothing his wolf and allowing Mason to track her to the kitchen. She sat at the kitchen table, engrossed in her phone, hair falling around her face and caressing her cheeks. He wanted to tuck those strands behind her ear and feel the softness of her skin against his fingertips. He stood there and just watched her. At least until she caught sight of him from the corner of her eye.

Her bloodcurdling scream probably made the sentries wonder exactly what the hell Mason was doing, but he didn't really have time to worry about them. Not when his mate reached for the knife block on the counter and whipped out the longest blade.

"What the *fuck!*" Yeah, she had a strong set of lungs.

Ignoring her, he stepped forward and placed the paper bag he'd brought onto the small kitchen table. He then went to the cupboards, opening and closing several until he found plates before hunting up utensils and napkins.

"I'm serious." She jabbed at the air. "That's it, I'm calling the cops."

In her panic, Lucy had dropped her phone, the small bit of plastic and glass sliding across the tiled kitchen floor. Unwilling to get too close to him, but still anxious to clutch the device, she half-crouched in a vain effort to retrieve the phone. Her fingers wiggled, mere inches from her "salvation." Mason chuckled and shook his head before he fished his cellphone out of his back pocket. He tossed it to her, and like a true alpha mate, her reflexes were so quick she caught it without so much as a fumble.

"In case you didn't know, the number is 9-1-1." Mason's smile widened. "Tell 'em Mason Blackwood is in your kitchen and you want to be assured the big bad wolf isn't going to eat you."

Mason snorted at his own joke because there was nothing he wanted to do more than taste his mate. To lie between her thighs and lick up all her sweet cream. She shot him an unamused glare but mostly ignored him and dialed quickly. He listened to her frantic—and pissed off—explanation of her "emergency" while he plated their food. His wolf drove him to care for her and its first step was making sure she was well fed. The deep rumbling voice on the other end of the phone could only belong to Jasper, a part-time 9-1-1 operator and full-time Blackwood pack wolf.

"Why the hell should I give a shit if he's a park ranger?" Lucy demanded. At least her anger was directed at someone other than *him*. "My house isn't in the fucking forest."

Mason tried not to grin.

"Trust you?" she yelled into the phone. "I'm supposed to just 'trust you' that he's a good guy? Even though he just *broke into my house?* Did I misdial and get the Mayor of Crazytown?"

Mason chuckled, and she shot him an irritated glare, which just had him smiling even wider. And why wouldn't he be happy? He'd found his mate—in the nick of time, too. Now he was caring for her, as was his duty *and* privilege. In fact, he'd never felt so at peace in his life.

"Are you going to send some cops out here or am I going to have to protect myself with this big-ass knife?"

More rumbling from the phone, which seemed to at least ease Lucy's fears, if not her anger. While setting the table, Mason made a mental note to give Jasper a bonus. Table as pretty as he could make it, he took the seat opposite the one Lucy had already claimed.

"Thanks for nothing, asshole!"

Lucy jabbed the face of the phone hard and that snarling glare was back on Mason. Her gaze shifted to the food, then Mason again, and back to the food. She took a deep breath and despite her anger, he knew he'd won this round. No one could resist this meaty goodness.

That's right. Smells good, doesn't it?

"And exactly what am I supposed to do with that?" She waved the knife at her full plate.

Mason picked up a rib and bit off a hunk of barbecue sauce-slathered meat. "Eat. Hopefully you'll enjoy it enough I'll get to hear a sexy moan."

"Perfect. You're an intruder *and* a horn dog. What a winning combination," she drawled.

She had no idea how close she was to the truth. With a smirk he grabbed her fork, scooped up some collard greens and held it out to her. "Eat. It's good for you."

"Said the man who broke into my house to force feed me."

Mason popped the forkful of greens into his mouth instead and swallowed. "See? I'm not trying to poison you. You're injured, and you need food high in protein and iron. Now sit."

Lucy hesitated, but soon the smell of the food overrode her remaining resistance. She retook her seat and laid his phone on the table between them. "I thought chicken soup was supposed to heal all ills."

Good, she seemed to be calming down. Getting all riled up was no good for her while she was injured. She favored her injured leg with every step, and he didn't like that blood had seeped through her bandage a bit.

"I'd rather watch you eat my meat," he smirked and gave her a wink.

Lucy's cheeks blazed red. She snatched the fork from him and took a bite of the greens. Unfortunately, she denied him the moan he'd been hoping for.

"Why are you *really* here?" She picked up a rib and gnawed on it.

God, that's hot.

"What do you mean?"

"I may not be familiar with every aspect of law enforcement, but I'm pretty sure a kid nearly getting run down in town by a clueless tourist doesn't fall under the Forest Service's jurisdiction."

Mason chewed slowly as he tried to come up with a reasonable excuse. One that wouldn't send her screaming for the door. "I was told a wild animal was involved and—"

Lucy interrupted him with a blast of noise that sounded as if he'd just guessed wrong on a game show. "Try again, Ranger Rick. The only animal was the fat cat the kid was trying to save. Cats aren't exactly wild animals."

Damn, she was impressive. Frustrating as hell, but impressive. She wasn't about to let him slide on his line of bullshit. What surprised him even more was the fact he liked it. Thank God his cell phone rang as she waited for his answer.

A big "NC" glowed on his screen. Normally, a call from the National Circle would elicit a grumble of irritation— as respected as the NC were, no alpha liked receiving a call from them—but under the circumstances, Mason had never been more relieved for an interruption.

"I have to take this." He snared his phone and pushed to

his feet. "Eat every last bite. Mine too, if you want. And throw out that nasty shit that's in the oven."

Lucy sputtered as he headed for the door, but he couldn't resist one last look back. When he caught her gaze, he tipped her a wink. "See you in the morning, sunshine."

CHAPTER SEVEN

THE COUCH CREAKED AS LUCY SHIFTED HER WEIGHT, searching for a more comfortable position. One that kept her leg elevated but didn't make her joints scream at her for sleeping on one side all night. All in all, she'd slept maybe three hours and not a single one had been restful.

After tossing and turning well into the night, a certain sexy park ranger refusing to leave her mind, her exhausted body had taken charge. It'd dragged her into the depths of sleep. Almost before her eyes had closed, bizarre and beautiful dreams had consumed her.

She slunk through low bushes and tall grasses, the underbrush teasing her face and shoulders while her ears remained lifted and listening for signs of life. The urge to chase throbbed inside her, maybe even kill. If she'd been awake, she would have been appalled, but not in her dream world. In her land of make believe and exhaustion, the need to kill couldn't have felt more natural.

All was silent save the crack of twigs snapping under her feet and a raven cawing from its perch high in the trees. The treetops swayed in the breeze, adding a rustle of leaves to the night music.

But the earthy smell of the forest startled her most. After her parents' deaths, Lucy had avoided wooded areas. The sharp bite of pine reminded her too much of camping as a family. Yet in her dreams, that scent felt like... home.

She sensed another presence behind her and she whirled, ready to bite the head off whoever—*whatever*—had snuck up on her. It smelled like an animal—feral musk mixed with crisp morning dew—but when she turned to face the interloper her breath caught. A naked man stood before her, but not just any man.

Mason.

The guy who'd barged into her life and demanded she answer questions he had no right to ask. The one who sent tingles through her when he merely glanced in her direction. The man she couldn't stop thinking about, though she'd rather gnaw off her own leg than admit that weakness.

She didn't need to ask what he wanted. Not when the evidence stood tall and proud, proclaiming to the world *exactly* what he desired.

Her.

In her dream world, Mason reached for her, his bedroom eyes filled with a deep craving that had her trembling, and she held out her hand in return. So, so close to one another and he stepped forward again and again until mere inches separated them. Electricity seemed to crackle between them, a hint of how explosive it'd be when they finally gave in to their bodies' needs. His fingertips brushed her and...

An orgasm wrenched Lucy from slumber, eyes popping open, back arched, and mouth dropped open while she sucked in a heaving breath. Wave after wave of pleasure danced through her body, ecstasy consuming her from head to toe. Her muscles were no longer her own, toes curling and pussy clenching as she rode out the last hints of pleasure. She trembled, a shiver of joy racing down her spine and then she huffed out a long sigh as she slumped against the couch once more.

Sleep beckoned her, urging her to return to that pleasurable dream-land, but she resisted the call. She knew she'd get sucked back into a dirty dream—one that went beyond a delicate touch—about the most arrogant and presumptuous man she'd ever met.

Don't forget sexiest.

With an exhausted sigh, Lucy pivoted on the couch until she was in something close to a sitting position. Her leg throbbed with the steady beat of her heart, which wasn't the best of signs. After she sucked down a strong cup of coffee and three ibuprofens, she'd call the clinic and set an appointment. Hopefully she would have enough strength in her leg to drive herself.

Of course, the moment she tried to stand, her leg told her she was an idiot. Searing pain shot up her thigh and straight to her brain then beyond to the moon. She groaned as the pulsating agony increased and gripped the bandaged area, hissing at the sensitivity of the wound beneath.

Lucy took slow, shuffling steps across the living room, and it took her a full five minutes to make it to the nearby kitchen doorway. *Fuck.* She paused and leaned her damp forehead against the frame while she rested for a moment. She stared at the familiar marks in the wood, the ones that read *Mommy 5'6"* and *Daddy 6'2"*. Today's emotional ache at the reminder of her parents was less than yesterday's. That was progress, right?

She took slow, deep breaths and prepared herself to move again, bracing for the pain to come. Only to have that bit of calm shattered by a heavy pounding on her front door.

How could she already recognize Mason's knock? Probably because he was the only person who'd visited her. Sighing, she half-hobbled, half-hopped toward the door, groaning and moaning with every hobbling step. She reached for the knob, metal cool against her palm, and twisted to grant him entry.

Except the doorknob sort of fell off in her hand. *The fuck?*

While she stared at the misshapen metal, Mason shoved the front door open and stepped inside. Lucy lifted her attention to Mason and then back to the useless doorknob before returning to Mason once more. Since she wasn't about to get answers from a lifeless—*useless*—knob, she'd interrogate this jerk.

"What the hell happened to this?" She waved the doorknob at him. "And why bother knocking if you're just going to break in anyway?" She snarled and hopped to her right, blocking his path.

Instead of answering, Mason jiggled the bag of groceries he carried and flashed her a shit-eating grin. "You could just give me a key and make it easy on both of us."

Lucy snorted. "A key to a useless knob? *Right.*"

She remembered that small town residents could be interfering, overstepping busybodies but this was too much. She opened her mouth to tell him where he could shove his idiotic request when she caught sight of heaven in a plastic package within his bag. Her stomach grumbled, not-so-silently begging for the pieces of ambrosia he'd brought.

Okay, she still wouldn't give him a key, but maybe she was acting a little too hastily. After all, the hottie brought *bacon.*

Bacon. Bacon. *Bacon.*

Rolling her eyes, she sighed and stepped aside to let him pass, but that wasn't what he did. No, instead, Mason stepped into her space, crowding her against the wall and surrounding her with his presence. And thank God for that wall because her knees went weak as soon as a wave of his scent passed over her. It was woodsy and spicy and musky, all wrapped together with a deliciously muscular bow—powerful yet subtle. Was it his cologne? Or just his natural scent? Whatever it was, it had to be loaded with pheromones. From the moment the first tendrils teased her nose, she got all hot and tingly in all the right—no, *wrong!*—places.

Mason moved until no more than an inch separated their bodies, his heat scorching her with his nearness. He lifted his free hand and gently cupped her cheek. The touch set her skin on fire and the throbbing ache in her leg sped up to match her racing heartbeat. Soft pressure had her tilting her head back until she had no choice but to meet his gaze. Something she absolutely *should not do* if she wanted to keep her sanity. And keep her panties in place. But there was she was, her eyes locked on his, those soft green whirlpools sucking her in and refusing to release her.

"How are you feeling?" His tone was soft, concerned.

Terrible! Whether you know it or not, you got me all hot and bothered in my dreams last night so it's your responsibility to fix it. We need a trip to Bangtown, STAT.

Lucy cleared her throat and fought to find her voice but only managed to whisper her response. "Fine."

A muscle in Mason's jaw twitched and then he nodded, releasing his hold—physical *and* mental. Free of his captive stare, she slumped against the wall at her back, digging her fingernails into the hard surface. He spun in place and then strode away from her, his heavy boots thudding against the wood floors. And all she could do was stare. Stare at that tight, firm, biteable ass.

No, bad Lucy. Bad.

Lucy wasn't able to stop drooling until Mason disappeared into the kitchen, giving her back what little sanity she possessed. She didn't like this guy. She didn't even *know* him. Not really. Sure, during her conversation with Miss Violet she'd learned Mason Blackwood had helped build Ashtown into a vacation destination.

That didn't mean he was trustworthy, though. Plenty of psychopaths fooled people into believing they were normal pillars of the community every day—politicians, religious leaders, Barney the Dinosaur…

No, wait. Barney just turned *others* into psychopaths as a form of self-preservation.

Lucy sighed and pushed away from the wall. As much as Mason tripped her trigger, she couldn't let her guard down. Not even to honestly acknowledge her feelings about the man. *Especially* then.

Resolve freshly renewed, Lucy hobbled toward the kitchen, wincing every time she put weight on her injured leg. Before she even made it out of the entryway, Mason appeared out of nowhere and scooped her into his strong arms.

"What the hell!" she gasped and shoved against his chest in a pathetic effort to get away.

He ignored her complaints and wriggling, and strode toward the kitchen. She jostled against his chest, all too aware of the hard plane of muscle she was snuggled against. That warm, natural woodsiness enveloped her like a cocoon once more. All she ached to do was breathe deeply and savor that scent. Unfortunately, all she could manage was frantic panting.

Even as she fought him, she had to admit that the handful of seconds it took him to reach the kitchen table were some of the most blissful in her life. Not that she would ever admit being held by him was so delicious and comforting, even to herself. She even managed to convince herself that her reaction was due to the fever she'd been fighting since the previous night. Of course, that lie she told herself was proved false when he set her down in a chair and returned to his bag of groceries. A fierce disappointment gripped her heart the moment he released her, and it wouldn't let go.

"So," she said, mentally slapping herself back into reality, "is this the new routine? You break into my house, carry me around, and cook for me?"

Mason lifted a single brow as he pulled a dozen eggs from the bag. "Would you like it to be?"

"Only if I could have a couple more servants to feed me grapes and fan me with palm fronds." Lucy laughed, just a little too brightly to be natural. The guy made her nervous. Sue her.

He turned and leaned one elbow on the counter as he gave her a sultry look, as if her every fantasy could be sated and all she had to do was ask.

Uh oh.

"You know I'm kidding, right?" She needed to get that out there. She didn't want Mason fulfilling any fantasies—real or made up. "I definitely don't want to you busting into my home every day."

She didn't care for the sly expression in his eyes, but he finally turned away with a barely audible, "Mmm hmmm."

Pulling a frying pan off the rack hanging over the kitchen island, he opened the package of bacon and began laying them in the pan. "How many pieces do you want?"

"None."

He froze and slowly turned to look at her in a mixture of utter bewilderment and horror. "You don't like *bacon?*"

Her tummy rumbled again, making her feelings about bacon clear. No sense denying it. "Okay, I love bacon, but

I can make it for myself, thank you very much. You don't need to—"

"Thank God," he blew out a harsh breath and dumped the entire pound into the pan. "For a minute there..."

"Listen, I really appreciate you bringing me food and all, but I'm perfectly capable of taking care of myself." Or she was at least perfectly capable of calling an Uber to ferry her around Ashtown. *Have credit card, will travel.*

"Really." It wasn't a question.

"Yes, *really*. I've been doing it since I was a teenager."

Mason's lips pressed into a thin line, forming a white slash beneath his nose. "Lucy, you're running a fever and you can hardly use your leg. You probably have an infection that needs to be treated. After I feed you, I'm going to take you to get checked out."

Wow, the balls on this guy!

"The hell you are!" She knew she needed to see a doctor, but she'd be damned if she was going to let him take all the credit for being a hero. Pushing down hard on the table, she managed to gain her feet... and she didn't even tumble over. Ha! Take that! "Mason—"

"How do you take your coffee?" He pulled jar of cold-pressed coffee concentrate from the bag.

Coffee sounded like heaven, but she balked just to be

stubborn. "My mother taught me to never take things from strangers."

"Light and sweet it is. Breakfast will be a bit, so why don't you go get ready."

"Why don't you get the fuck out of my house?" Fury at him—and herself—pumped through her veins.

Though that anger was sorta tempered by the fact that she appreciated his attempt to take care of her—a nobody from nowhere who he didn't know from Adam. Not one of her past boyfriends had ever looked after her when she was sick. One or two had managed to bring her soup on the first day of her illness before skittering off to do something more interesting. After that, she'd always been on her own. But boy, when *they'd* caught so much as a sniffle, they'd expected her to wait on them hand and foot. Hence the *exes*.

A low sound from outside caught her attention. It was barely there, maybe nothing more than a whisper on the wind, but she swore it sounded like laughter.

"Lucy," Mason slapped the wooden spoon down on the counter, "you're sick. You'll feel ten times better after a hot shower. Right now, you have two options. You can be a good girl and take a shower on your own, or..." His eyes darkened, his green eyes looking almost amber for a moment. God, she really was sick. But even sick, she could appreciate the rumbling purr in his voice. "I can help you."

He grinned and waggled his eyebrows at her, sending a

rush of heat to her cheeks. To cover her embarrassment, she barked out a contemptuous laugh.

"Oh, I'm totally gonna hop in the shower with a stranger in my house. This may be a small town, but assholes aren't restricted to big cities. Dickheads can be found in the country too, you know." She waved a hand in his direction. "Case in point."

Mason opened his mouth—probably to argue though she was determined to win this confrontation—but then his nostrils flared and he turned toward the hallway. Lucy didn't have a chance to ask him what he'd heard when a female voice echoed down the hall.

"Knock knock! Anyone home?"

The sound of little feet running quickly followed, and Charlie skidded around the corner into the kitchen. "Hi!"

"Hi," Lucy grinned at the little boy, bemused by his sudden and unexpected appearance.

Charlie rushed up to her, glancing briefly at the dried blood on her sweats before launching into a rambling lecture on, well, *everything*.

"Morning! We came to see you! Does your leg hurt? I feel really, really bad. I didn't mean to. I was just scared. And Ghost Kitty was going to get *run over*! I wanted to save her, even though I know I'm not supposed to like kitties. I was worried about her all night, but then on our way here, I saw her again. In your front yard! She's so fat! And really cute. She's grey and looks really soft. And fat! I want to pet her. I asked Mommy and Daddy if I could keep her, but they said I was too young. I won't hurt her like I hurt you though, I promise. I'll be really good. Is that bacon?"

"Charlie, leave her alone," his mother chided.

Bonnie and Robert Tipton followed their son into the kitchen, stopping short when they spied Mason at the stove. Bonnie shot her husband a glance soaked with worry, but then she was all smiles and open arms.

"Mason!" She smiled wide and welcoming. "Bless my stars, I wasn't expecting to find you here."

Robert pumped Mason's hand and leaned in, the move followed by the two exchanging low murmurs she couldn't hear. Mostly because Charlie had started in about the cat again. All the commotion and activity brought on a wave of dizziness that sent her plopping into her seat. She remained in place and simply waited for Charlie to take a breath.

Lucy put her elbow on the table and propped her cheek against her palm. She sighed and tried to follow the action in her kitchen. Why she was surprised by this, she wasn't sure. This was small town Georgia, after all, where everyone was always in everyone else's business. Couple that with a healthy dose of guilt and the ever-present "bless your heart" Southern attitude, and it was no wonder strangers invaded her home. After so many years on her own, all the attention made her feel somehow... loved.

Lucy brushed the thought away with a shake of her head and focused on Charlie's prattling. "...but she ran under your porch before I could get her. I hope she's okay under there. Do you think cats are scared of the dark?"

"Charlie Tipton." Mason's stern tone reverberated around the room and everyone stopped talking, moving, breathing.

Charlie turned slowly, almost in slo-mo, dropped his gaze to his toes and shuffled over to stand in front of Mason. The Tiptons stood off to the side, clutching each other's hands in a white-knuckled grip, practically trembling with nerves.

"What do you have to say for yourself, young man?" Mason's voice was dropped low with a hint of growl.

A shiver of dismay wriggled up Lucy's neck, standing the fine hairs there on end. Charlie gave a small shudder before answering. What the hell? She couldn't make sense of the scene. It almost appeared as if they all were kowtowing to Mason. Good grief! He was just a park ranger, not a general!

"I'm sorry," he mumbled, eyes still focused on the floor. "I'm sorry for hurting Miss Lucy."

The boy glanced over his shoulder at her, and she gave

him a soft smile to let him know there were no hard feelings.

Mason interrupted their moment. "And?"

"And…" Charlie whispered. "And I promise never to bite anyone again."

"What was that? I didn't hear you."

Charlie's lower lip trembled, and his chest hitched as he bravely fought the tears. Anger bubbled inside Lucy. If *she* had been able to hear Charlie, Mason had. He was just being a jerk. She couldn't believe his parents weren't putting a stop to this nonsense. If they wouldn't, she would.

"That's *enough*." She lurched from her seat and stumbled until she formed a human barrier between Mason and Charlie. She jammed her fists onto her hips and glared up at Mason. "Why don't you pick on someone your own size, you big bully! Besides, how is this any of your business in the first place?"

The Tiptons gasped and Charlie whimpered, but she ignored them. She was determined to set Mason on fire with her glare. It didn't work. Apparently, she still wasn't a superhero. The only thing her snarling accomplished was to amuse the gorgeous man. No, she meant asshole. He wasn't gorgeous. At all.

"And what are you grinning at?" she demanded.

He raised his hands in surrender and smiled even wider while taking a step back. "Not a thing."

She snorted and rolled her eyes and then turned to Charlie. She leaned down—kneeling so wasn't happening —and smiled at him. "Apology accepted, Charlie." Then she glanced at his parents. "Thank you for coming to check on me, but I'm fine."

"But your leg—" Robert started, but Mason cut him off.

"I'm taking Lucy to get the wound looked at just as soon as she gets cleaned up."

She turned her glare up to eleven, but he still remained stubbornly incombustible. And grinning.

"Or rather," Mason added, that grin somehow widening, "as soon as I *help* her get cleaned up."

Ass. Hole.

CHAPTER EIGHT

THE OLD CHEROKEE BOUNCED DOWN THE RUTTED STREETS of Ashtown, each jarring movement drawing sharp breaths from Lucy. The Jeep's lurching obviously bothered her leg, but he couldn't do much about the condition of the road. And the situation was only going to get worse. The road to the pack house could be confused with the cratered surface of the moon. Yeah, she'd hate him by the time they arrived.

Lucy's unique, distinctly feminine scent wrapped around him like a warm blanket fresh from the dryer. His wolf grumbled at Mason's restraint in claiming their mate, but he shushed the animal. Rushing things might scare her off. Matings between humans and wolves weren't completely unheard of, but humans didn't sense the fated mate connection as strongly as wolves. Once they received the mating bite and transformed, everything was peachy.

Until that moment, it was a crapshoot and Mason wasn't big on gambling.

Of course, *everything* about the situation was a crapshoot because she'd been bitten by Charlie instead of her mate— him. A bite from him would have bound them forever and her transition from human to wolf would have been painless and spiritual. A human getting bitten by a random werewolf almost always led to death.

His wolf howled its objection and he struggled to quiet the beast once more. It refused to even consider the possibility of losing Lucy. Not now, not ever. The animal told Mason he *would* do *everything* in his power to keep their mate alive. Period.

At the moment, Mason only had hope. Hope that Charlie's underdeveloped powers, and the fact Lucy was fated for Mason, would lead to a happy ending for everyone. They wouldn't know until her transformation was complete, which left Mason in a heightened state of anxiety. And the phone call he'd received while Lucy had been showering didn't help matters.

Bonnie had helped Lucy shower and get dressed while Robert and Charlie went hunting for a phantom cat, which left Mason to his own devices. After tidying up the kitchen, he'd wandered from room to room, hoping to pick up bits of information about his mate. He knew her name, her address, and that she had enough backbone to make a fine alpha mate, but that's where his knowledge ended. So, he'd poked around a little.

It wasn't as if he'd been *snooping*. Alphas never snooped. Of course, while he had been *not*-snooping he'd realized the house wasn't *hers*. Photos of her were scattered all over the downstairs level. There was an image of her blowing out eight candles on a big birthday cake that sat in a silver frame on the mantel. Then a collage of a teenage Lucy acting silly with friends that took up most of a wall. Even an adorable shot of her as a baby, lying naked on a fur rug that was hung proudly on the wall leading upstairs. They were cute and allowed him to see into his mate's past, but they weren't photos a woman would hang in her own home.

Another hint was the house itself—dated décor and an odor of neglect. Not dirty, just... stale. The home had stood frozen in time—filled yet empty. Why? If she didn't live in the house on Maple, where *did* she live? He had so many questions, but he filed them away until the time was right.

Veering sharply left, Mason maneuvered the Jeep onto an even rougher road. He slowed to a normally frustrating crawl, but he was in no hurry to get back to what—or rather *who*—waited for him at the pack house. He much preferred Lucy's company, even if she'd barely said a word since clicking her seatbelt into place.

"Doing okay?" he cut his gaze over to her and noticed that the hem of her pretty little sundress had inched up her thighs, giving him a view he would have enjoyed thoroughly if not for a big square of bloody gauze.

She continued staring out the window as she spoke. "I've never been out here before."

"Not many have." And there was a reason for that. Not that he could tell her… yet.

"Strange," she hummed. "I'd always thought my parents had taken me camping or hiking over every square inch of this mountain."

"So, what do you think?" He refused to admit that butterflies took up residence in his stomach. Alphas didn't worry about anyone's opinion.

She released a heavy sigh. "It's beautiful."

Mason let out the breath he'd been holding, thankful that Lucy loved his pack lands as much as him.

"And those wildflowers! I've never seen so many in the forest before." Lucy cranked down the window to catch a whiff as she turned to smile at him for the first time.

Wonder and joy lit her face, transforming her from merely beautiful to absolutely breathtaking. It certainly was a good thing she liked the place that would soon become her home. Because that was one hundred percent going to happen. She just didn't know it yet.

"My grandmother planted those before I came along," Mason explained as he turned onto an even narrower road. "She could never remember which turn to take to get home. My grandfather bitched and moaned about them, but he stopped every week when they were blooming to pick a big bouquet for her."

"That's so sweet," she mused, craning her neck to watch the flowers for a moment longer.

"We Blackwood men have a way with women, as you've seen."

Lucy snorted and barked out a laugh. "Yeah, real smooth." She took a deep lungful of the fresh mountain air and sighed happily, closing her eyes and resting her head on the doorframe as the sun warmed her face. With a start, she turned to him again. "Does your family own all of this?"

"Yup," Mason said proudly. "For generations. I've lived here all my life and I can honestly say I know every inch of this forest."

"Well, you *are* a park ranger."

He shrugged. "That wouldn't matter. I knew this mountain long before I joined my father in the Parks Service. He and my grandfather taught my brothers and me everything about caring for our mountain. How the flora and fauna work together to create a healthy ecosystem. We're just stewards of the forest, and we take that responsibility very seriously."

"You really love this place, don't you?" she asked softly, her curious gaze probing his profile.

"More than you can possibly know."

For now, he added silently.

The gentle moment was interrupted by a child's shriek and a loud howl. Mason glanced out Lucy's window to see Danny Spade running as fast as his four-year-old legs could carry him. He screeched again with delight when his father, Colin, bounded out of the underbrush in his wolf form. He nipped at Danny's bare butt, which made the kid giggle higher and run even faster. Mason smiled, recalling how his father used to chase him and his brothers around the forest in the same way.

"Stop!" Lucy scrambled for the latch to her seatbelt. "Stop the truck!"

Mason instinctively looked around for danger but saw nothing. "What? Why?"

She turned wild eyes on him. "Don't you see? That rabid dog is going to kill that little boy! *Stop the fucking truck!*"

Mason braked hard, not because he was worried about Danny but because Lucy already had her door half open. Mason was out and around the truck before she managed to untangle herself from the seatbelt and climb down. He helped her the rest of the way, concerned about how little weight she could put on her leg.

"That's not a rabid dog. It's a wolf," he tried to reassure her, but she pushed him away and crouched down to grab a big rock.

"Jesus! Whatever, I'm not letting it eat that poor baby!"

Mason did his best not to laugh. She was rightfully scared, as any human would be. Still, he couldn't resist teasing her a little.

"And you're going to stop it by throwing a rock at it?"

She shot him a dark look and then let the stone fly. It didn't even come close to hitting the completely oblivious Colin, who was still chasing after his squealing son. She stooped and grabbed another.

"Lucy—"

"First, you're an asshole. If I can get its attention, it'll leave the boy alone and come for bigger prey."

Mason sighed. Part of him was frustrated because he couldn't tell her the truth, but another part of him was impressed she would sacrifice her own safety for a member of the Blackwood pack. Another sign she would be an outstanding alpha mate, but he wished she'd wait until she was healed to be so amazing.

Lucy's second rock bounced off the wolf's head and she shouted at Colin. "Come and get me instead!"

Colin spun, hackles raised along his spine. He dropped his head low and flashed sharp, white teeth in a dangerous snarl.

Great.

Mason stepped forward and only had to say one word. "No."

Colin's glowing amber eyes shifted from Lucy to Mason. His eyes widened slightly and then his hackles laid down and his ears folded back in supplication to his alpha. Lucy took the opportunity to hobble forward as fast as she could and scoop up Danny into her arms. She limped back to the truck, glancing over her shoulder at the wolf the entire way.

Watching her cuddle the boy to her chest gave Mason a vision of what she would look like holding their own pup. Her maternal instincts were just as good as any wolf mother, and he couldn't wait to get started making their first.

Colin's gaze darted between Mason and the strange human woman holding his son. He was clearly torn between protecting his child and obeying his alpha, as any good father would be.

She won't hurt Danny, Mason told Colin using their connection as pack mates.

What makes you so sure? Colin wasn't quite trusting all was well.

Because she's my mate and she will soon be your alpha mate.

Colin's eyes grew wide and he broke out into a wolfy grin, tongue lolling out of his mouth. He yipped and did a twisting backflip in celebration of the news the entire pack had been waiting for. Their alpha had found his mate and the pack would be saved!

Lucy cringed at Colin's antics, so Mason urged Colin to chill, at least for a bit.

"He won't hurt you or the boy. He's tame. They were playing," Mason told Lucy.

She didn't look entirely convinced, but Colin slinked in close and sat at her feet, panting up at her happily. Danny squirmed in her arms, reaching out for his father, but Lucy refused to put him down. Mason could hear her heart beating fast, but the sharp smell of her fear was fading quickly.

"Are... are you sure?" she asked, flicking a wary gaze at Mason.

"Positive."

To prove his alpha's point, Colin nudged Lucy's good leg with his snout. The physical contact nearly sent Mason's wolf into a frenzy. But when Lucy reached out to lightly stroke the animal's forehead, Mason fought to control his own urge to grab Colin by the throat and fling him into the woods. He'd never imagined he could so jealous of a shifted wolf.

Sensing his alpha's agitation, Colin took a few steps back and turned his amber eyes on Mason.

The National Circle has arrived. They're waiting for you at the pack house.

Mason sighed. Exactly what he'd been dreading since Roman called to inform him they were on their way. It hadn't helped that they wouldn't tell him the cause of their visit. He assumed it was about the fire, which was a topic he'd happily put off thinking about. Regardless, his primary concern was seeing to Lucy, and there was only one person who could help.

Is Drew here yet? he asked Colin.

The wolf nodded his furry head. *And the National Circle seemed very interested in talking to him.*

Mason frowned. *Why?*

Colin gave a wolf version of a shrug. The news agitated Mason. If the NC wanted to talk to Drew, they weren't here about the fire at all. They couldn't have possibly heard about Charlie and Lucy so quickly, but it had to be something big for them to travel all the way from Ft. Lauderdale.

"Come on," Mason said to Lucy, "the house is just around the bend. We'll take the wolf and the pup with us."

He opened her door and ignored the curious glance she gave him as he helped her and Danny inside. He'd called the boy a pup on purpose, wondering what her reaction would be. Curiosity was good. Concern about his sanity wouldn't have been.

"Dr. Cooper is waiting for us," he said as she got settled. "He wants to have a look at your leg."

Colin jumped into the back, his head poking between the front seats. When he gave Danny a playful lick, the kid squealed and clambered out of Lucy's arms and snuggled into his father's warm fur.

Lucy shook her head. "And tell me again why I'm being seen by a vet?"

Mason ignored the question and focused his attention on being so close to his mate. After securing her seat belt, his fingers drifted up her side until they reached her face. Cupping her cheek, he stared deeply into her soft blue eyes and breathed in her heady aroma. He couldn't hold back for a second longer.

Leaning in, his lips pressed against hers, gently. She stiffened at first, not pulling away but not participating either. Then his wolf howled with joy as she relaxed, leaning into his touch. He resisted the urge to kiss her properly, delve into her and discover all of her secrets, but he was all too aware of the child and wolf in his back seat. Breaking off the kiss long before he was ready, he pulled away and pressed his forehead to hers, latching on to her gaze with his.

"You're seeing Drew because I said so," he finally replied.

Without waiting for her reply, he shut the door and headed around the front of the truck, adjusting his fully erect cock along the way. All worries about the fire and the National Circle flew from his head. All he cared about was getting Lucy healthy so he could claim her so fiercely, so completely, that neither of them would be able to walk right for a month.

CHAPTER NINE

Lucy clenched her teeth against the urge to cry out from pain. The truck continued to bounce over the rutted road, eventually rocking to a stop in front of an absolutely ginormous log cabin.

She stared out through the windshield, gaze scanning the massive home. The wolf and little kid clambered from the vehicle. The duo darted across the yard, child giggling while the wolf barked and yipped. She'd been so foolish jumping from the truck the way she had and chasing after a little kid who didn't want—or need—to be saved. She'd never heard of a four-year-old having a wolf as a pet, but stranger things had happened.

When she'd seen the beast tearing after little Danny, memories had come flooding back—memories she'd spent years suppressing. She hadn't been able to save her parents, so she damn well was going to save the boy. Now her entire leg throbbed in a never-ending cycle of agony because of her foolhardy bravery.

The rapid movements stirred up the infection overtaking her flesh. The heat radiating off the leg left no doubt that infection had settled in nice and deep. When she'd undressed for her shower, she'd discovered a wide circle of red spreading out from the bite marks. She needed antibiotics, and maybe some pain meds. Strong ones.

"How're you doing?" Worry etched Mason's brow.

For a split second, she was tempted to rub her thumb on the crease there to ease his concern. She shook her head to clear away the ridiculous thought and flashed a smile instead.

"I'm okay. I could use some help getting down, but I think I can walk on my own." She hoped he didn't call her out on the lie.

The moment her feet touched the ground, the door to the massive house opened and three men filtered out, as if they'd waited for her to move before exiting. Each one appeared more foreboding than the last as they lined up on the porch. They simply stared at them, remaining in place and not coming down to meet them. A rather pale Dr. Cooper emerged last and stood a short distance away from the other men.

"We have a welcoming committee," she quipped to Mason, wincing as she took a step. "Only they don't look very welcoming."

Mason ignored her comment and wrapped a strong arm around her waist. As much as she hated leaning on him, she was grateful for the support. The lodge tilted sideways, and she wondered why it didn't float off the edge of the earth. The men on the porch were so far away and then they were close—nearly standing on top of her. Then the ground lurched and the cabin bounced back into place. Huh. It was all so odd and yet... wasn't.

"That the victim?" the tallest of the three strangers asked no one and everyone. He had longish dark hair and brilliant green eyes that reminded her of a freshly mowed lawn. *Pretty.*

Mason drew them to a stop at the foot of the steps and gave a curt nod. A vein pulsed at his temple and Lucy could almost hear his heart beating. Scratch that, she could *actually* hear his heart beating. It thumped so loudly she wondered if the others could hear it too. *Thud. Thud. Thud.* Then came the *whoosh* of blood in his veins.

"What's the prognosis?" one of the other men, who could have been Chris Hemsworth's twin, spoke to Dr. Cooper.

Drew shot her a worried glance and then shrugged. "Normally, I could give you a definitive answer, but this is a... special situation."

Lucy's gaze bopped from one man to another, trying to figure out what the hell they were talking about. They kept looking at her, but she was no victim. Unless... They couldn't be talking about Charlie biting her, could they? Dear Lord, these people took a kid biting someone way too seriously. Some children were just *biters* at certain ages. Charlie just had a behavioral problem to sort out.

As the thought flitted through her fevered brain, the rascal in question peeked around the corner of the lodge. All the men were oblivious of the boy's presence, but Lucy caught his eye. She smiled and gave him a flirty little wink, bringing a big grin to his face. Then Mason turned to see what she was staring at and Charlie disappeared.

Cute kid. If her own kid turned out half as sweet, caring, and rambunctious as Charlie, she'd be thrilled. A vision of her lying in bed, holding her newborn baby while Mason wrapped his arms around them both shocked her back to reality. She had no idea where the image had come from, but this was no time to be fantasizing about a happily ever after. Not with a man she didn't really like, much less actually *know.*

"We can discuss it later," Mason growled at the men, taking a step forward.

The three men didn't budge, effectively barring the way inside the lodge. Mason's sudden movement caused Lucy's vision to swirl. She clutched at his bicep, barely even noticing how bulging and big it felt under her fingers—barely.

"Lucy!" Mason cried out and the next thing she knew she hung limply in his arms. She hardly had the strength to twine her arms around his neck. *How very damsel in distress*, she thought with a snort.

"Out of the way," Mason demanded, pushing past the men whether they liked it or not. Their glares said they were definitely in the "not" category.

"We need answers, Mason," one of them spoke—Lucy couldn't tell which with her faced pressed into Mason's neck.

"You'll get them, just not right now." Mason's growling voice felt way too good. All snarly and vibrating and *yummy*.

Lucy wanted to call them all assholes—couldn't they see she was sick?—but speaking required energy and she had precious little.

The most she could handle was to loll her head around and take a peek at Mason's home. Beautiful handmade log furniture decorated the place, giving it a welcome, homey feel. Several couches and dozens of chairs created a huge seating area, which puzzled her. Either Mason lived with a *bunch* of his relatives or he lived in a hotel.

Heavy footfalls on wooden floors reverberated against wooden walls until Mason kicked open a wooden door. His distinct scent hit her stronger than a room full of fragrant roses. It suffused the air and seemed to be embed in every inch of the space. He'd obviously carried her to his bedroom. He tucked her under his covers, and she almost fainted from his heady, woodsy musk. She didn't understand how this stranger could make her... *want.* When he pressed his lips to her forehead, Lucy had the sudden urge to tilt her head back until their lips met. The kiss would be hesitant at first but it wouldn't take them long to dive into the growing desire that existed between them.

The thudding of multiple pairs of feet broke the spell, drawing Mason's attention from her and to the room's entry. He stood in front of her, legs spread and arms crossed. The three men from the porch stopped at the doorway, and Mason took a threatening step forward.

"Not another inch." There he went with the growling thing again.

The one who looked to be the leader of the trio clenched his jaw and gave Mason a dark look. "Don't fight us on this, Mason. We're the National—"

"I know you're the fucking National Circle, but I'm the fucking alpha of the Blackwood pack and I will *not* have three unmated alphas in here with my mate!"

Squinting hard at Mason's increasingly blurry back, Lucy replayed his last words in her head, just to make sure she'd heard them correctly. Alpha? Pack? Mate? Who was his mate? *Her?*

What the everloving fuck?

Lucy tried to sit up a little, shifting her weight and begging her muscles to comply. She groaned at the rush of pain that came with the movement, but she was determined to ask them what the hell they were talking about. Drew chose that moment to appear at her side and pressed a cool hand to her blazing forehead. He frowned and then turned to Mason and jerked his head toward the doorway. Mason gave her one last glance before herding the three men down the hallway, closing the door in his wake.

Drew reached for the gauze she'd wrapped around her leg after her shower, tugging on the material and yanking a hiss from her mouth. "*Fuck* that hurts."

"I know," Drew soothed, "but I need to check out your wound."

Lucy ground her teeth to stop herself from sounding like a big baby over a little bite. She kept her eyes focused on the wooden ceiling, counting the knots in the wood as a distraction. Only when Drew gasped did she look down at her leg and sucked in a harsh breath to match his. What'd been a few gouges was now a throbbing purple and red gash.

"Holy shit," she whispered. "This morning it was just... Is this because I jumped out of the truck?"

Drew ignored her as he pressed the edges of the angry injury. Air whistled between her teeth with each new wave of agony, but she didn't cry out again. She managed to remain silent. Barely.

He continued to poke and prod, eyes scanning the twisted

wound. Finally, he looked up at her, a grave expression in his grey eyes. "I need to grab a few instruments." Drew abandoned her and went to the door. "Don't move, okay?"

"Couldn't if I wanted to," she mumbled, closing her eyes and immediately falling into a drowsy state.

Mason's voice filtered through the wall behind her, barely audible at first, though it grew louder with each passing second. Strange because it seemed as if he was trying to whisper. The more she listened, the more clearly she could hear his voice—but not the others. She wondered how her hearing could be so strong when the content of the conversation blew away all other concerns.

"If you're not here about the fire, why *are* you here?"

The other men's voices mumbled so quietly she could barely pick them out, but then Mason's burst in her head like a bullhorn.

"A tip? What kind of tip? About what?"

More murmurs, and then Mason cursed so loudly she winced.

"You've got to be fucking kidding me! Frank-fucking-Riverson set fire to *our* pack lands, but you're here to investigate an illegal change?"

Lucy didn't care that she couldn't hear the others. Mason's words were still pinging around inside her brain. *Werewolf?*

"For fuck's sake, it was an accident! Do you really think I sic one of my own pack's pups on a human woman just to grow our numbers? Who called in that tip?"

Pack? Pup? *Human woman?*

If Lucy had thought her heart was racing before... No, she couldn't have possibly heard correctly. The only answer was that she was delusional. That had to be it because she sure as shit wasn't listening to four grown men talking about being werewolves!

Lucy didn't hear Drew approach, but she sensed his presence. When he reached toward her leg, she shot her hand out and locked onto his wrist in a death grip. Only then did she open her eyes to stare into his surprised face.

"Drew, please don't think I'm crazy, okay?"

His brow pulled together in a frown. "Okay."

"Do you know..." She paused and listened hard to make sure the lunatics in the next room were still babbling at each other. "Mason and those other guys... they all think they're... *werewolves?*"

Drew's eyes grew wide as saucers and his breathing became shallow. Great, he thought she was the crazy one. Squeezing his wrist as hard as she could, she tried again.

"I know, I sound insane or delusional or something, but I swear to God they're talking about it in the next room. I know you're buddies and everything, but you seem like a really good guy. *Please* help me get out of here. I can't end up like some too-stupid-to-live bimbo in a bad horror flick!"

A shadow dropped over Drew's eyes, but instead of helping her up and out of the Little Lodge of Horrors, he took a deep breath and shouted, "Mason!"

Perfect, just perfect. As the sound of his crackpot leader's feet running up the hallway thundered through the lodge, Lucy wondered if she should give them some tips on the best way to season her for their evening meal.

CHAPTER TEN

MASON STRODE INTO HIS BEDROOM, SCANNING THE ROOM for any threats. Lucy lay in the bed, fists full of blanket and eyes squeezed shut, body tense as she braced for oncoming pain. Drew stood at her side, a wicked-looking instrument in his hand. That was the moment Lucy's eyes popped open and she met his stare across the distance. With her panic-filled gaze came a wave of her scent—the sweet notes now crowded by the stinging hint of fear.

His wolf howled and demanded its release. It would eliminate the threat against their mate. Permanently. But Mason had one problem with obeying the wolf's desires— he didn't see a threat, only Drew.

Drew, the healer.

Drew, the unmated male.

Drew, the man Mason had left alone with Lucy.

Having never had a mate, Mason was nearly knocked off balance by a ferocious surge of jealousy. He glared at Drew, lungs hardly able to draw in air. The man he'd trusted to care for his mate must have done *something* for her to be so fearful.

Mason crossed the room before Drew could so much as blink and wrapped his fingers around the healer's throat. With the merest flex, he slammed Drew against the wall, the wolf's feet dangling two feet above the floor. The other male's hands scrabbled at Mason's wrist, but he refused to release his prey.

Only Lucy's scream stopped him from breaking Drew's neck. He spared a moment to glance at the bed and met her terrified eyes. The scent of her panic filled the room with a cloying stench that drove him mad, drove his wolf toward the edge of violence. No doubt about it, whatever had scared her before he entered was nothing compared to how she felt as Mason pinned Drew to the wall.

Common sense told him that the only difference between then and now was *his* presence. It was enough to break through his hormone-fueled rage. He lowered Drew to his feet though he refused to release the wolf. He stared into the man's wide eyes.

"What did you do?" Mason growled through clenched teeth.

Before Drew could speak, Lucy answered for him with a

snarl of her own. "Nothing! Except for not answering my question."

Mason's fury lessened while apprehension crept in. He released Drew and turned to face his mate. Who didn't know she was his mate. Or that he was even a werewolf.

"And what question might that be?"

She narrowed her eyes and her nostrils flared. "Whether he knew you nutjobs think you're werewolves."

Mason stopped breathing, and he was pretty sure his heart stopped beating as well. *Shit!*

He hadn't wanted her to find out this way. She would eventually have to learn the truth about the Blackwood pack, and her eventual membership, but he'd wanted to ease her into their world slowly. How had she discovered their secret? Drew?

No, it hadn't been the healer. The wolf was loyal to the pack above all. In truth, Lucy's accusation was no doubt the reason why Drew had called for Mason.

"What makes you say that?" Mason kept his tone cautious, soothing.

Even in her sickness, she had enough pluck to roll her eyes at him. "Seriously? I heard you talking in the next room, plain as day." She pointed a trembling finger at him, the shakes revealing her weakness. "Don't even try to deny it."

He wouldn't call her a liar about hearing the conversation, but he could easily have denied that their meeting wasn't next door. Mason had escorted the National Circle through the pack house and back to the sitting room to have their little chat. No human could have heard their mumbles at that distance, much less any details.

A spark of hope joined his rolling fear. She exhibited symptoms of transforming into a wolf—the only question was whether she could survive the transition. No matter what, Mason was going to do everything in his power to ensure she lived.

He returned his attention to Drew and wrapped an arm around his old friend's shoulders. He walked the healer to the door and Drew didn't need to be told to leave. Drew gave Mason an encouraging nod and then left the room though Mason knew he'd stay nearby, ready to help when he was needed.

The National Circle waited nearby, the trio's gazes not leaving Mason. He kept his voice low as he spoke. "Time to leave, gentlemen."

The beta and the enforcer backed away, but Roman—the alpha of alphas—didn't budge. The other two glanced at each other and then followed Drew, leaving Mason and Roman to face off on their own.

Mason ground his teeth as he glared at Roman. National Circle Alpha or not, Mason wasn't about to allow him anywhere near Lucy. "You need to leave. *Now.*"

To his credit, Roman kept his cool, but the way he crossed his arms made it clear he wasn't leaving any time soon. "I'll leave after Miss Morgan has answered a couple of questions."

Defying the National Alpha would normally earn a wolf all sorts of painful punishment, but the only thing that mattered in that moment was Lucy. A growl developed in his chest, but a feminine snort jolted him out of his growing anger. Both he and Roman glanced at the bed where Lucy remained, a firm glare in place.

"You can go suck a lemon, pal," Her objection endeared her to Mason even more. "I'm not answering questions until I get a few answers of my own. Do you freaks really think you're werewolves, or what?"

Mason bit his lips to keep himself from smiling. He'd known she was one ballsy chick even before they met— throwing herself into the path of an oncoming car to save a child proved that—but seeing her tell off the National Alpha was more than he could have dreamed. Judging by the frown Roman gave Lucy, he disagreed though Mason caught the gleam of amusement in the man's eyes.

Lips twitching ever so slightly, Roman returned his attention to Mason. "We're not leaving until we have answers, Mason."

The last of Mason's patience evaporated, and so did his inhibitions about speaking freely in front of Lucy. Even if they left the room, she'd hear it all anyway. She'd already proven that fact.

"Listen," Mason jabbed a finger in the air in Roman's direction. "I have an injured mate who's asking questions, and she has a right to answers. I don't need to remind you how this could turn out. Instead of taking a step back, you're more concerned about bleating like a fucking sheep over a mishap involving a young pup!"

"I'd stop pointing if I were you," Roman's jaw worked overtime and his green eyes flashed a dark warning.

"And if I were *you*," Mason curled his lip. "I'd figure out who called in the tip in the first place. Interesting timing, don't you think? That you got a helpful call about the Blackwood pack breaking laws at the exact same time I'm dealing with an asshole starting fires in my forest. Convenient, don't you think?"

Roman examined Mason for a moment before he spoke. "Seems as if you already have a theory. Share with the class."

That was the alpha of alphas—demand, not ask.

Mason didn't care for the man's condescending tone, but this wasn't about only him anymore. This involved Mason, Lucy, and the entire Blackwood pack. The National Circle needed to know his thoughts, if they didn't have suspicions of their own already.

"Word spreads fast in small towns, Roman. Frank

Riverson free of jail for more than an hour before I heard about his release through the grapevine. I'd be pretty fucking surprised if he didn't have a whole lotta hate for the Blackwoods. After everything that happened, wouldn't you?"

Roman scowled. "How did you—"

"Never mind all that," Mason interrupted. "In addition to the fire, the pack house was vandalized. Two days *after* Frank's release."

"You never reported that."

"I know. At first, I thought it might be local kids from town, no big deal. After the fire though, it didn't take a genius to put two and two together. I was preparing an official request for an investigation by the NC when all of...*this* happened."

He waved a hand back toward Lucy but kept his eyes laser focused on Roman.

"Now you get some mysterious tip there's some massive conspiracy involving our pups biting humans to grow our ranks." Mason huffed in frustration. "You *must* see what's going on here, Roman. You can't possibly be that dumb."

Roman's upper lip pulled back in a warning snarl and Mason had just enough control to not snarl back. The scent of Lucy's fear had increased steadily as the two men spoke, and he'd do just about anything to be alone with her so he could calm her. He should placate the National

Alpha, keep the man happy, but Lucy needed him more than Mason needed to kiss ass.

Out in the main living area, Mason could hear his brothers talking to Roman's beta and enforcer. Plastering a fake smile on his face, he motioned toward the door.

"Listen, I'll gladly talk about this until we're all blue in the face. *Later.* Right now, I've got a mate to claim and that requires privacy. Got it?"

Roman's gaze shifted between Mason and Lucy and back again. With a nod, he finally left them alone.

CHAPTER ELEVEN

To Lucy's hypersensitive ears, the click of the door latch catching sounded like the metallic thud of a prison cell slamming closed. Even worse, it *felt* like a death sentence. Oh sure, the big house in the middle of nowhere was filled to the rafters with smoking hot men—and not just regular hot, but a-nun-tearing-off-her-habit hot—but on the flip side, they all thought they were werewolves. Had she mentioned she was alone with them? In the middle of God's nowhere? Awesome, right?

Mason snared a chair and dragged it toward her side of the bed. Lucy's gaze darted around the room, searching for a weapon—some way to defend herself from the crazy. With Mason's strength and speed, she'd never make it to the door before he caught her. Her only hope was that someone had inadvertently left a bazooka lying on the bedside table.

No such luck.

Mason spun the chair around and straddled the back. So very manly. So very sexy. His green eyes burrowed into her, making her skin crawl in the most pleasurable manner. Even as sick as she was *and* as nutso as he was, the heat between them threatened to engulf her.

This is how girls in horror movies die, dummy!

Right! She'd almost forgotten she was trapped in a house with a bunch of crazies. If she'd learned anything from scary movies, it was to never walk into a dark room after hearing a child-like giggle and to always play along with the bad guy's delusion. He might cut someone in half with a chainsaw if they didn't.

"I won't taste very good, you know," she blurted the words out. "Not even Gordon Ramsey could make Lucy Stew taste good with all the infection in my body. There's puss and goop and icky creepy crawlies in my blood. I'd probably give you food poisoning."

Mason's laugh started out soft, then his belly joined in, and soon it was rumbling up from his toes. At the sound, a good portion of her fear evaporated like a puff of smoke on a windy day. He wiped a tear from his eye and grinned down at her.

"I'm sorry to disappoint you, but you're not on the menu for dinner. We don't generally eat humans, and not just because we're half-human ourselves."

Lucy's fear should have surfaced again, but there was nothing but calm in Mason's presence. It gave her the courage to ask questions that might have challenged an otherwise insane person's beliefs.

"So, you're…"

"A werewolf." Mason didn't hesitate to answer. Nothing but a hard certainty in his gaze.

"Uh-huh." Lucy was doubtful and hesitated to ask him anything else. Don't poke the crazies, right? Even the hot crazies.

He cocked his head slightly, like a curious dog—er, wolf. "Even if you believed every word I said, that can't be your only question."

Curiosity overpowered Lucy's remaining wisps of fear. Even though the idea of werewolves—like, *real* werewolves—was completely ludicrous and beyond imagining, this was a golden opportunity not many people would ever have. To ask a "real" werewolf questions normal people often had, such as…

"Okay, I'll bite," she smirked when she caught the meaning of her words. "So to speak."

Mason's expression didn't change. He simply sat with his forearms resting on the back of the chair, eyes on hers as he waited patiently. Though a part deep down inside Lucy sensed he was anything *but* patient.

"Are werewolves born or made? Every movie I've ever

seen suggests they're all made. Someone goes *nom, nom, nom* and boom, werewolf. But if that's how they're made, how was the first werewolf created? Movies don't address that." She frowned. "Talk about a plot hole," she grumbled.

"First of all, don't believe everything you see in movies," he winked. "Second of all, we're born this way. Usually."

"Usually?"

Mason's attention turned to the lamp on the bedside table instead of at Lucy. "There are very rare occasions when a wolf's bite can transform a human into a werewolf."

Lucy narrowed her gaze. He'd chosen those words so carefully. *Too* carefully. "Do you mean it's rare for a wolf to bite a human, or that it's rare for a human to survive a wolf bite?"

Mason shifted in his seat and cleared his throat. "Both."

A deep sense of foreboding settled on her. More vague-speak. He wasn't telling her something. Something that was obviously important, or he wouldn't avoid spilling the beans. It was just a matter of asking the right questions.

"In what situation might a human survive a wolf's bite?"

He finally met her gaze again. "When they're fated mates."

Heat pooled in her cheeks at the mention of mates. He'd seemed to be calling her that earlier. Did that mean he was going to try biting her? Anything could happen when someone was fully committed to their delusion. Maybe shifting topics would keep his mind off biting her neck.

"So, who are the surly dudes? Psycho, Rando and Thor?"

"Psycho must be the alpha, but what's a Rando?" Mason asked, clearly puzzled by the slang.

"You know, random brown-haired dude? Rando?"

His chuckle sent a whisper of warmth through her. "So, you think Dane looks like Thor?"

Lucy shrugged and then winced as the simple movement brought a fresh wave of pain from her leg. "A little. Now quit stalling. Who are they?"

"They're the National Ruling Circle, headquartered in Ft. Lauderdale, Florida. Psycho's actual name is Roman. He's the National Alpha. Rando is Silas, Roman's beta—the second in command, or for mafia movie buffs, his consigliere. Thor is Dane, the enforcer. Basically, he's the head of security."

"I don't get it. What do they have to do with you?"

Mason scratched an eyebrow as he thought. "Let me backtrack a bit. All wolf packs have a Ruling Circle made up of an alpha, a beta and an enforcer. The alpha is sort of like the president, the beta most resembles the judiciary, and the enforcer is congress."

Lucy couldn't stop herself from giving him a little verbal

jab. "So, you're telling me your leaders are all incompetent nincompoops, too?"

Mason laughed, and once again, Lucy felt a comfort and ease she'd never experienced. For some reason her logical mind couldn't fathom, his mere presence made her feel safe. Safer than she'd felt since the day her parents had died. In fact, she wanted to ask him to lie down next to her and wrap his arms around her, but she managed to control herself. Barely.

"I'd like to think we care more about our people than politicians," Mason said when he caught his breath, "but you never really know what's in someone's heart." He paused and stared deeply into her eyes. "Do you?"

The urge to invite him into her bed grew stronger. Lucy swallowed hard and pressed on, ignoring what her body demanded.

"So why are they bugging you? You're the alpha here, right?"

Mason held her gaze a moment longer before answering. "I am, but every pack in the country falls under the purview of the National Ruling Circle. You could think of the packs as states and the NRC as the federal government."

Lucy rolled her eyes but said nothing more.

"Roman and his men are here to investigate a false claim

that someone in the Blackwood pack violated our code of conduct."

"How do you know it's false?"

"I just do."

"Uh huh," Lucy mused. "So, everyone in this house is a werewolf? Even Drew?"

"Drew is the pack healer, which is why he's qualified to treat you."

"He's not just a vet?"

Mason's smile lit her world on fire. "Nope."

"Well, that's a relief." To her surprise, it was true. Almost as if she was starting to believe all this werewolf nonsense. Then another thought hit her. "Good lord, is everyone in Ashtown a werewolf? What about Miss Violet from the coffee shop?"

"As human as they come."

Lucy smiled, happy that one of her favorite people was just like her. But that disquiet she'd been battling with surged to the surface and a thought popped into her head that made her blanch. "Wait, what about Charlie?"

What remained of Mason's smile flitted away, replaced with a grim expression. "The Tiptons are members of my pack, including Charlie."

"But…" She thought hard, trying to fit the puzzle pieces

together. "But if Charlie is a werewolf, and he bit me, then…" She turned wild eyes on Mason, true fear pulsing through her, especially the spot the boy had bitten. "Am I going to die?"

Mason reached out and took her hand in both of his, stroking it gently. "We don't know for sure. You're something of a special case."

"Why?"

"Charlie might not be your mate, but you are destined to be mated to a werewolf."

"How do you know that? How can you be sure?"

The worry in Mason's eyes softened to something else. Something Lucy wasn't ready for. "Wolves know their fated mates the moment they meet," he explained. "The connection is instant and forever, but it isn't until they mate fully that their bond is unbreakable. I knew we were fated before I even laid eyes on you. I smelled your scent on Drew and my wolf recognized you as our mate."

Lucy stared at him blankly for a moment. "Now what the fuck do you expect me to say to *that?*"

He smiled again, melting her from the inside out. She couldn't deny she was attracted to the man. *More* than attracted. She was drawn to him on a cellular level. Her body yearned for him, ached for him, needed him to survive.

That's it!

"So, if Charlie isn't my mate—obviously—but you are, then what happens? Will... whatever you call it... *mating* me save my life? If so, what are we waiting for? Don't let me die, Mason."

"Never!" His upper lip pulled back in a snarl that in no way felt threatening to Lucy. Quite the opposite. She understood instinctively he was growling at the possibility of her death. "But it's complicated, Lucy."

Tears burned her eyes and she turned her face away from him. "Whatever. This is all a bunch of bullshit anyway. You're not a werewolf and I'm not dying from some stupid bite from a little kid. I'm just hallucinating all of this. That has to be it!"

"You need proof." Mason's tone was cool and confident. Lucy turned back to him, ignoring the tears streaming down her face unchecked as she nodded.

Without a word, he pushed himself out of the chair and moved to the center of the room. He dragged his black t-shirt over his head, revealing the contours of his chest. A fine spray of hair dusted his pecs, but what lay under the hair had Lucy swallowing hard and fast as he unzipped his jeans. When he hooked his thumbs in the waistband, she closed her eyes—partly to give him privacy, partly to control her own wildly erratic libido.

"If you want proof, you need to open your eyes, my love."

Gripping the bedsheets in her fists, Lucy pried open her

eyes. Mason stood proud as a peacock, his entire, fantastically ripped body on full display for her.

And only her, something deep inside her growled.

Then Mason wasn't quite Mason. He lengthened and became broader. The hair on his chest thickened and spread across his entire body. His face stretched, and before she could even blink, Mason wasn't Mason at all.

Before her stood a giant wolf, its fur so dark it was almost black, but with a faint hint of brown—just like his hair. Fangs poked out from its snout. Sharp claws clacked on the floor as it settled into its new form. Its fluffy tail wagged. But the creature's eyes caught Lucy's attention. Green as a springtime field—Mason's eyes.

Even as the room spun around her, and the world faded to black, Lucy understood in her soul that werewolves were real.

CHAPTER TWELVE

MASON DIDN'T TAKE HIS ATTENTION FROM LUCY AS DREW left, the healer quietly closing the door behind him. Mason had summoned the healer the moment Lucy lost consciousness and Drew... had been less than pleased at Mason for shifting. Even now, the words continued to flutter through his mind.

"She's fighting for her life, Mason," Drew scolded him. "Next time you want to impress your mate, do it when she's healthy, okay?"

Mason slumped in the chair by her bed, wishing Drew had given him a chance to explain. He'd only wanted to give her the proof she'd needed, but inside he knew the truth. He'd wanted his prove himself worthy to his mate. He'd wanted to show her his wolf and parade around for his mate.

Listening hard, he could just make out the conversation between his brothers and the NC. Kade and Gavin invited them to the main dining room for dinner, which was just fine by Mason. Roman, Silas and Dane might be his superiors, but nothing would come between him and his mate.

Lucy became restless and whined in her sleep, the sound not stopping until Mason clasped her hand. She sighed and settled just as he suspected, his touch calming her. Maybe lying next to her would ease even more of her discomfort.

Mason had slipped on his boxer briefs after returning to his human form. While he normally slept in the nude just in case he needed to shift on the fly, he crawled under the covers with them on to keep himself from going wild with desire for his mate. He gathered her in his arms and pulled her into his body, realizing his meager efforts were futile. Her curves fit into his hard planes softly and perfectly, making his body react in an instant without restraint.

It took hours for him to fall asleep, and one dream occupied his mind all night—claiming Lucy. His exhaustion so deep from hardly any sleep, not even the sun streaming through the windows woke him the next morning. No, that honor was reserved for children squealing with delight as they ran up and down the hallways.

Mason cracked open one eye and groaned as he squinted

into the brightness of the room. He'd forgotten to close the blinds the night before and while the sun seared his eye, the brightness at least gave him a good view of Lucy. They'd shifted around in their sleep until she now lay on her side within reach. A fact he'd somehow taken advantage of during the night. He'd slung his arm protectively around her waist. Her skin glowed—flushed pink in a way that reminded him of passionate nights tangled in the sheets and he went hard in an instant. Only for a soft groan to bring him back to earth and bathe him in shame for lusting after her while she fought for her life.

Mason snuggled closer, careful to keep his cock away from her tempting, heart-shaped ass. Lucy stiffened in his arms, body ramrod straight and tense. He brushed his lips across her temple and she relaxed into his embrace with a soft sigh.

"Good morning," he whispered in her ear, enjoying the way her body shivered in response. "How are you feeling? Do you need anything?"

Her voice was scratchy with sleep. "No, but I think you might need to be committed."

His laugh rumbled up from someplace soft and deep within him. He barely knew Lucy, but he could tell that his heart was already half hers. Maybe more than half. The simple fact they were fated mates didn't always equate to insta-love. That developed slowly like any relationship, and Mason was thrilled he already sensed its effect on him. He couldn't ask for more in a mate—she was beautiful, good and strong, and had a wicked sense of humor.

Pulling her closer, he enjoyed the way her body fit into his, even though she felt far too hot to the touch. His wolf even settled down, reveling in the closeness of their mate, even though the beast in him was desperate to claim her. Not yet. She was too ill.

"How did you sleep?" he asked, breathing in her scent like she was a batch of freshly baked chocolate chip cookies.

"Weirdly." A little furrow formed between her eyebrows. "Pretty sure there was more howling, fur growing, and chasing of rabbits than usual." Yeah, he was falling for her all right. Had already fallen. "It must have been one of the eight thousand shots Drew gave me last night."

"Do you have any questions about what you dreamed? Such as how mates—"

"You can stop right there," she interrupted, pulling away from him a little. "This mate stuff is just a little too...." She paused for a beat and shook her head. "I need some space to think, which is hard to do with you pressing your dick against my business."

Mason hadn't even been aware he'd moved. He shifted his hips backward and buried his face in the spray of her hair. "I'm sorry. I can give you space, but I'm not letting you out of my sight. You should know that up front."

Lucy sighed dramatically. "Do I need to hit you with one of the forty-seven pillows on this bed?"

"I'd like to see you try."

"If I had more energy, you'd see what I was capable of. I'm lethal in a pillow fight."

Mason grinned at her sass. "Challenge accepted. As soon as you're feeling better, that is."

He let her deflect away from the subject of mates... for now. They had much more to discuss, including the fact that while he would happily give her "space" on the matter, he wasn't about to let her out of his sight. Not only was she potentially deathly ill from a non-mate wolf bite, but Frank Riverson was out there, just looking for a way to hurt Mason.

Mason wrapped her in his arms, and erection or not, pulled her so close their bodies almost melded into one. She sighed and relaxed in his embrace, and they lay there for a long, luxurious moment, just breathing in each other's scents. He was a split second away from spinning her around so he could stare at her full, luscious lips when someone knocked loudly on their door.

"Probably Drew," Mason groaned, as he hauled his ass out of bed.

Mason dragged on his jeans, struggling to stuff his cock into the uncomfortable constraints of denim. Then a fresh scent hit him—from Lucy. It wasn't her illness, or even the panic he'd smelled on her far too many times since their first meeting. This was sweet and pungent, full of passion. It was the smell of his mate's desire for *him*. He hesitated, torn between fulfilling her desperate need and giving her space as she'd requested. The persistent knock on the door made up his mind for him.

Mating would have to wait.

Still, he couldn't stop a smile from spreading across his face at the knowledge that Lucy wanted him as much as he wanted her. The smile fell away, though, when he opened the door and came face to face with his brothers and Drew.

"What—" he started to ask, when Charlie Tipton shoved between the men's legs, dragging little Danny Spade behind him.

"Miss Lucy!" Charlie cried as he pushed past Mason and ran for Lucy.

Mason sighed in defeat. Clearly his alone time with his mate had come to a screeching halt. No point in barring the men from entering the room, so he threw it open and moved quickly to intercept Charlie and Danny before they could dog pile on top of Lucy. Grabbing them both by their waists, he plopped them into the chair he'd used the night before and scooted it toward the foot of the bed.

"There," he told them, "now you two can talk to the alpha mate without getting in the way of the healer."

Lucy gave him a sharp glance at the mention of alpha mate, but he just grinned at her. She could deny it all she wanted. He knew the truth and wasn't about to dismiss their connection.

Without a word, Drew set to work checking on his patient while Charlie talked a mile a minute, carefully holding a squirmy Danny in his lap.

"I saw Ghost Kitty again today," he reported to Lucy, and to her credit, she gave him all her attention. Probably better than looking at the needles Drew shoved in her veins.

"I thought she was under my porch," Lucy said.

"Me too! She must like you. I saw her crawl under the porch of the pack house this morning."

"Really?"

He nodded profoundly. "Yes. And she was *so* fat!"

Lucy chuckled, pointedly ignoring Drew's activities. "No wonder she's hiding from you. No lady likes to be called fat."

Charlie's eyes grew wide and concerned, and his bottom lip wobbled as if he might burst into tears. "Do you think I hurt her feelings?"

Lucy's sweet smile nearly burst Mason's heart. "I don't think it's anything an apology couldn't fix."

Without a moment's hesitation, Charlie slid off the chair

and helped his little buddy down before scuttling from the room, calling for Ghost Kitty. "You're not fat! You're so pretty, Ghost Kitty! Please come out and play!"

The sound of little feet pattering down the hall finally faded, and Mason turned to Drew. "How is she?"

Drew said nothing, but Mason caught the way he pursed his lips and the troubled expression in his eyes. The healer didn't need to use words for Mason to know what he was thinking.

Not good. Not good at all.

"It's time, Mason," Drew said quietly.

Lucy's alarmed gaze bounced between them. "Time? Time for what?"

"Are you sure?" Gavin asked Drew, who shrugged in response.

"No. I've never dealt with a situation like this before. My best guess is that she has a better chance of surviving this if Mason claims her sooner, rather than later."

All eyes turned on Lucy. She panicked and scooted away from them under the covers.

"Um, you know what? I'm suddenly feeling so much better. I think all I really needed was a good night's sleep."

"Lucy," Mason spoke softly, trying to calm her before she freaked out.

"No!" She glared at them in turn.

Drew, Kade and Gavin all looked nervously at Mason. For the past few months, he'd been unpredictable with a constant edge of violence. He understood their concern but now that he'd found Lucy, any trace of that feral beast that had once plagued him had vanished. His only concern, from now until death, was Lucy.

"No! You guys are nuts!"

"But Lucy," Mason said quietly, "you saw me shift last night."

She shook her head wildly, like a little kid throwing a tantrum. "I don't care! It was a dream!"

With a glance from Mason, the others left them alone, closing the door behind them. Dropping to his knees next to the bed, Mason reached out and cupped her burning hot cheek and hoped he could show her everything he needed to say in a single touch.

CHAPTER THIRTEEN

LUCY QUIVERED AT MASON'S TOUCH.

Quivered.

Even as she pressed her hot cheek into the cool roughness of his palm, she cursed herself as twelve kinds of a fool. The guy was clearly off his rocker, not to mention the fact he was practically a stranger, and yet…

His effect on her was undeniable.

She'd never felt anything like it before. All her past boyfriends paled in comparison—almost faded from memory entirely. If asked, she would have been hard pressed to even remember their names, much less how they'd made her feel.

But werewolves? her logical brain insisted. It wanted her to remember that he believed he was a *werewolf*.

Everything that had happened since Charlie bit her was colored by the sickly glaze of infection, but Lucy knew deep down she had witnessed Mason shifting from human into a wolf. As much as she wanted to pretend she'd been dreaming—*hallucinating*—she knew the truth. Werewolves existed.

"Lucy?" His gravelly voice was a tonic to her frayed nerves. She sighed in response, every cell in her body yearning to trust him, despite what her silly brain told her. "There are things we need to talk about, but I don't want to scare you."

Her eyes fluttered opened and she tried to smile, even though her body felt as if it was weighted down by a metric ton of rocks. "I think we crossed that line when you turned into a ginormous wolf."

He let out a relieved breath and rubbed his thumb against her cheekbone. "Okay, here goes. I've been waiting for you my entire life, Lucy Morgan. I didn't know it, not until yesterday, but that's the truth. You're the reason I'm still breathing. You're why I'm still alive and sane."

Her arched eyebrow made him chuckle, which sent a shiver of joy through her aching body.

"Okay, as sane as someone like me could ever be," he corrected, before continuing. "Until you came along, I fully expected to be put down by year's end. Now I have the chance at a future I'd never dreamed possible. You're my miracle, Lucy, and no matter the outcome, I intend on having my mate by my side."

It took a few seconds for Lucy's brain to process his words. When his words finally untangled themselves, she frowned. "What do you mean, 'put down'?"

A muscle in Mason's jaw flexed. "As far as unmated werewolves go, I'm getting long in the tooth, so to speak."

She smiled, only because she didn't have the strength to laugh. "So?"

"So... werewolves must find their mates at some point or another, or they'll turn feral."

"Why?"

Mason smiled softly at her, sending ripples of desire through her. "A mate soothes you, calms your wolf. Without that calming influence, the wolf starts to take over."

"And that would be bad?"

"Very. I was already losing control when we met. My wolf had been steadily taking control of our shared body more and more over the last few months. Everyone in the Blackwood pack knew it, but they were also patient, hoping I'd find my mate before..."

Lucy didn't like that he'd trailed off like that. "Before what?"

Mason sighed. "Before I lost control completely and the

rest of the Blackwood ruling circle were forced to *eliminate* the problem."

The severity of what Mason had been facing hit her like a Mack truck. "Damn, I thought being single in the human world sucked."

Mason smirked and stroked her cheek again. Lucy wouldn't have minded dying right then, if he'd just keep stroking her so sweetly.

"You are, quite literally, the other half of my soul, Lucy. I can't live without you. And now that I know you a little, I don't think I'd want to. I need you to believe that."

She met his very serious and very intense gaze. She should have scoffed at his words. She should have grabbed her cell and dialed 9-1-1 and "ordered pizza," as all the Facebook memes suggested. She should have run screaming through the woods until someone came along to round up all the loonies in that particular bin.

But something in his expression eased her doubts, and a scent she'd never smelled before soothed her, made her trust him. It was crisp and clear, like a sunny morning at the beach. It smelled pure and ancient and *right*, and it told her every word coming out of his beautiful mouth was the truth.

Since when did she smell *feelings*? Maybe it was her infection, or maybe her sanity. Whatever the reason, she trusted Mason as she'd never trusted anyone before. And more than that, the funny, fizzy feeling inside her belly every time she looked at him felt distinctly like love. Not like an anemic, soda pop "love" she might have thought she felt before, but like a rocket launching into space.

"I do believe you," she whispered, reaching up to lay her hand on top of his. "At least, I'm trying to. It's all just a bit much. I need a little time to come to grips with all of this. Maybe when I'm feeling better…"

Mason closed his eyes and kept them closed for a long moment. She didn't need any special ESP to know he was trying to figure out how to break some bad news to her.

"You have no idea how much I'd like to give you all the time in the world," he finally said.

"So why don't you?"

"Whether you can believe it right now or not, you were destined to become an alpha mate, Lucy. As a human, my mating bite would have transformed you painlessly. Since Charlie bit you, we have no idea how your change will go."

Adrenaline surged into her system as panic took hold. "Transform? Change?"

Mason winced, as if he'd forgotten to tell her a key part of the story. "When a wolf bites a human, one of two things happen. Either they die, or they turn into a werewolf themselves."

Lucy's mouth went dry, and no matter how much she tried to form words, nothing came out.

"We were all hoping it wouldn't happen, but it's pretty obvious Charlie's bite transmitted enough saliva to... infect you, for lack of a better term. Since you were fated to be my mate, it's still possible you could change on your own, but Drew thinks it would be safer—and more pleasant—if I claimed you right away."

As much as she enjoyed the feel of his hand under hers, Lucy pulled away and pinched the bridge of her nose, desperately trying to remain calm enough to make sense of all the craziness Mason had just lain in front of her. She took five deep, cleansing breaths, just as she'd learned in yoga class.

Didn't work.

"And what's involved with this claiming process?"

Mason leaned back and took his comforting hand with him. Lucy suddenly felt as if a part of her body had been removed. He stared at her for a moment before explaining. "When fated mates find each other, they bite each other on the neck... while they're making love."

Lucy let her eyelids fall shut. Her body burned so hot she shuddered with chills. Every muscle, every joint, every inch of her skin *hurt*. She'd never been so miserable in her life. The thought of making it all go away quickly was mighty appealing, but the very idea of exerting enough energy to have sex—even though every cell in her body screamed for Mason—quite literally exhausted her.

Besides, she was still not sure about all this "fated mate" mumbo-jumbo.

Turning to face him, she gave him her most pleading look. "Couldn't you just give me a little nibble now, and I'll take a rain check for the rest?"

CHAPTER FOURTEEN

MASON HAD NEVER APPRECIATED HOW MUCH COULD change in twenty-four short hours. The day before, he'd been fretting over his human mate's potentially mortal injury. Just last night he'd bitten Lucy in an attempt to heal her. Now the day after and they strolled down the sidewalks of Ashtown, window shopping and people watching. Since he'd begun his campaign to turn the town into a tourist destination, there was no shortage of either.

"I think you should grow a beard like that guy," Lucy said, nodding toward a fellow skating down the opposite side of the street.

The guy stood as tall as Mason and had twenty pounds on him. Beyond that, he sported a bushy, yet perfectly trimmed beard all the way down to mid-chest. Bright yellow dandelion flowers dotted the brown beard. He also happened to be wearing pink Hello Kitty skates.

Mason arched an eyebrow at Lucy, drawing a giggle from her. He loved the sound of his mate laughing. It meant she was alive and would continue living for the foreseeable future. He had no doubt that if he'd waited to give her the bite only a mate could administer, she would have died from Charlie's accidental bite. He was still in awe of her bravery in the face of certain death, but it just proved to him that she would be the perfect alpha mate.

Now they just needed to actually... *mate*.

As much as his wolf was pushing him to claim her fully, Mason wouldn't rush her. He had to set aside his innate alpha instincts and allow her to come to terms with a metric shit-ton of new information, an entirely new way of living. He could be patient... for a little while.

In the meantime, he simply enjoyed the feel of her fingers entwined with his and her new scent. It was her flowery aroma, only amplified a thousand-fold. They walked past tourists and, time after time, the strangers would turn their heads to watch her pass. Almost as if they smelled her new commanding power as well.

"How are you feeling?" He pulled her closer to his side.

She smiled up at him. "Fit as a fiddle. The wound was scabbed over and barely pink when I got dressed. It hardly hurts. I never thought I'd say this but... thanks for biting me."

Her fingers feathered across the tender spot on her shoulder where he'd sunk his teeth. Her shirt covered the evidence, but Mason could feel her pulse beating just under the healing skin. She hadn't yet shifted into her wolf form, but he sensed it building. Drew's best guess was that her body had to fight off Charlie's infection first, and then the transformation process would continue as any other. But since none of them—not even the National Circle—had any experience with this situation, it was anyone's guess how long it would take for her to recognize him as her mate.

As they strolled, Mason wasn't only "people watching," but he was also watching people. The NC could bury their heads in the sand all they wanted, but he knew Frank Riverson was behind all the fuckery going on lately. He continually and systematically scanned the crowds, holding onto Lucy's hand, just in case he needed to pull her to safety. Across the street, behind them, and in front of them, Mason's own sentries prowled the streets too, watching for any sign of trouble.

"I can't wait to bite you again," he murmured just loudly enough for her to hear.

Her cheeks grew bright pink and she shot him a mock glare.

"I'm just sayin'," he said, basking in her embarrassment. "I can't wait until you feel well enough to cash in that rain check. To fuck you into oblivion. To sink my teeth into my mating mark on your neck. To join you when you shift for the first time. To run with you in the woods, our paws pounding in time on the spongy earth."

Lucy grew quiet and listened intently, though her face still burned red.

"You won't believe the sense of freedom, Lucy. It's a joy like you've never experienced as a human. And I'll be by your side through it all, watching and supporting you as you discover your new self and get to know your inner wolf."

He lowered his voice. "And can't wait to feel your body under mine. Your breasts straining against my chest. Your creamy thighs opening for me. Your heat on my tongue. To claim you as my mate, forever and ever amen. Then you'll know what a mating bite *should* feel like."

Her scent shifted toward desire. His words were having the intended effect, even though he knew they couldn't just drop down on the sidewalk and go at it. But sowing the seeds of passion might yield a helluva bounty once they returned to the pack house.

"What do you mean?" she squeaked.

He stopped and skimmed a finger down her cheek and neck to the curve that flowed into her shoulder. She winced from the sting of the bite he'd given her.

"A mating bite shouldn't hurt. Not in a painful way, as it did yesterday. Only in a 'Ooh, baby, that hurts so good' kind of way. Under normal circumstances, mating bites are given during the course of, ya know, mating."

He pulled her against his body, wrapping his arms around

her lower back so he could rest his hands on her fine rump. Lucy relaxed into him and laid her hands on his forearms, staring up into his eyes.

"So, when you're ready, you just let me know in whatever way you see fit. Whisper it in my ear, take my hand and lead me to the bedroom, stuff your hand down my pants… whatever. I promise to blow your mind, but I won't push you."

Lucy blinked up at him, and he almost thought she would jump him right there on Main Street, but she finally nodded curtly and turned away. He sighed as he followed, but he didn't lose hope. She would be his, of that much he was certain. It was only a matter of time.

"I'm starving," she finally said.

"I'm not surprised. Your body is undergoing a massive change. That's bound to make anyone hungry. What'll it be? A big ol' country breakfast? A burger and fries? It is just about lunchtime."

Lucy shook her head and stared at a neon sign that featured a giant ice cream cone across the street. "Ice cream." She grinned. "A mountain of it."

Mason smiled in return. "You got it."

Once the street was clear of vintage Citroëns, Volvos and Saabs, Mason led her across the busy street and straight into Dickey's Diner. The proprietress moved as if on autopilot, yanking two plastic-covered menus from a holder on the counter and turning to them without really seeing them.

"Welcome to Dickey's Diner," she droned in a crusty monotone. "Take a seat— *Oh* hello, Mason."

Agnes Dickey was a stout, unflappable woman with enough grey hair to prove just how much her sons had put her through during their teenage years. Nothing fazed her anymore. Her husband Arthur—a thin, cheerful man— smiled through the pass bar between the kitchen and the dining room.

"Hey, Mason," Arthur called, before he turned back to whatever he had been cooking.

"Your usual?" Agnes pulled an order pad from the pocket of her apron.

"Not today, Agnes. Just ice cream."

"Sure. Pistachio for you, and for…?"

"Oh, I'm sorry. Lucy, this is Agnes and Arthur, the owners of this fine establishment. Agnes, this gorgeous woman is Lucy." He paused a beat for effect. "My mate."

Agnes' eyes flew open so wide Mason worried her eyeballs might pop right out. Though no one except his brothers had spoken with him about his… *situation* directly, everyone had known he'd been on the verge of going feral.

"Y-your…" She glanced at the humans enjoying their

meals to make sure none could hear as she whisper-yelled. "Your *mate?*"

Mason grinned.

Lucy glared.

Then Agnes did the most unexpected thing. She ran out from behind the counter and wrapped Lucy in a giant bearhug. Laughing and grinning and chattering like a happy little bird. Agnes handed over their ice cream and insisted it was on the house. Another first. A few minutes later, Mason led Lucy to a bench in the park downtown.

"That was low, even for you," she said grumpily as she licked up a drip of chocolate truffle ice cream.

Mason shrugged. "You're just trying to delay the inevitable. Besides, I'm proud to call you my mate."

Lucy blushed furiously and then tried to change the topic. "She sure was happy to hear the news. What a hugger!"

"You have no idea what an honor she just bestowed on you, fair maiden. I didn't even know she could smile before today. The woman didn't even tear up at her oldest son's wedding—and he was the favorite!"

"Well, I just hope she can keep her mouth shut."

Mason leaned back, giving her a satisfied smirk. "Oh, Agnes isn't known for her discretion. In fact, she has quite a reputation as a world-class gossip."

"What!"

"Yup. By nightfall, everyone in the pack should know you're my mate."

"B-but why?" Lucy stuttered.

"Eh, it's easier than telling everyone individually."

"You sneaky son of a—"

"Is that any way to talk to your mate?" He gave her a cocky little wink.

Lucy rolled her eyes. "You can't know for sure I'm your… you know."

"Mate."

"Whatever. You can't be certain."

"Of course, I can. Wolves mate for life. You're still transforming, which is why you still have doubts. Once you've fully changed, you'll understand that you're mine forever. You just don't know it yet."

Lucy's expression changed, softened into sadness. "Nothing is forever, Mason. One day you can be living your life, happy as a clam, and the next… it's over."

Mason didn't care for her fatalistic tone. "Sounds like you're speaking from experience."

She stared off across the park, lost in her thoughts, her past. "I learned the truth a long time ago."

"What truth? When?"

"The day my parents died."

Mason remained quiet, letting her choose how much to share. He wouldn't pressure her. As it turned out, he didn't need to. With a deep breath, she launched into her story.

CHAPTER FIFTEEN

"Hurry up, Lucy Goosey!"

Lucy rolled her eyes, sighed dramatically, and jammed a bookmark into the paperback she was currently obsessed with. It was artistic and darkly romantic and full of angst, just like her. The stupid camping trip her parents insisted on taking was seriously messing with her reading time.

"It's the last time we can go camping as a family until next summer," her mother had wheedled over the previous week until Lucy had agreed.

God, she couldn't wait to go to college and finally be free!

Stuffing her book into her backpack, she glanced around the room to see what she was forgetting. Her phone sat on her desk, and despite her parents' sacred rule forbidding electronic devices on their camping trips, Lucy grabbed it anyway. As of last month, she was officially an adult and they couldn't say boo about it.

"Besides, they should be grateful I'm going at all," she muttered to herself as she muted the ringer and tucked it into the pack's front pocket next to her pepper spray keyring.

"Luce!" her dad shouted. "Get a move on!"

"Coming!" she shouted back. "Jeez!"

Three epically boring hours later, her folks set up camp while Lucy sulked on a nearby stump. Dad had popped their old tent up in seconds flat, but he seemed to be having trouble with the new one they'd bought on the way out of town. Lucy had insisted she was too old to sleep with her parents in a pup tent and said she'd just sleep under the stars. Naturally, her overprotective mother wouldn't hear of it. Too dangerous.

Lucy had rolled her eyes and stared out the car window. Didn't they realize she could take care of herself? Besides, the wildest animal they'd ever seen on one of their trips was a raccoon who tried to pry open their ice chest once. And let's get real, what kind of protection did a thin layer of nylon offer against anything that really wanted to eat her? But she'd played along and picked a tent the color of blood. It reminded her of her book.

"Ta da!" her father cried, grinning from ear to ear and waving his arms around like a magician who'd just pulled a bunny out of hat.

Her mother clapped and cheered over his minor accomplishment and then turned back to the fire she was trying to start. "Failing" would have been a better word, but Lucy kept her snarky lips clamped shut. She loved her parents—really!—they were just so freaking clueless! They had absolutely no concept of how hard it was to be a teenager, what kind of pressures were heaped on Lucy's shoulders. Maybe one day they'd grow up and realize that the world wasn't all butterflies and unicorns, although she had a sneaking suspicion that their annoying optimism would never fade.

"Congratulations," Lucy muttered, rolling her eyes again as she threw her pack over her shoulder and crawled into the blood red tent.

With one deft movement, she zipped it shut behind her. Yanking her book from her pack, she lay back on a thin foam pad, using her pack as a pillow, and escaped from her boring, bourgeois life. Before the story had fully captured her attention, she heard her parents murmuring quietly, and she knew they were talking about her "bad attitude" again, but she didn't care.

Really!

The next thing Lucy knew, she woke up to the sound of twigs cracking nearby. She could barely see her hand in front of her face it was so dark. She must have fallen asleep reading, and since the sun didn't set till almost nine in her part of the world, she guessed it had to be closer to ten.

Righteous indignation flared inside her. Her parents hadn't even bothered to wake her for dinner! And they knew how much she enjoyed her mother's camp stew. Jerks! She ignored the twinge of guilt over acting like such a brat earlier. They should have at *least asked if she was hungry. The fire still crackled quietly, but she'd been camping enough times to know it had burned down very low, probably almost to embers.*

Maybe her mother had saved some food for her anyway. Lucy reached for the zipper, when she heard twigs cracking again and paused. If her dad was taking a leak, she certainly didn't want to accidentally see that, *so she waited until he went back into their tent. But he didn't.*

Or it didn't.

Whatever was prowling through their campsite didn't sound human. First of all, she could have sworn she heard four feet shuffling along instead of two. Plus, her father didn't huff and snuffle like a dog sniffing someone's crotch. Or growl.

Goosebumps spread across Lucy's arms and she froze in place, terrified to even blink. She had no idea what was out there, but the dim glow from the dying fire showed a silhouette of something big. Very big. A wolf, maybe? Suddenly she was very happy her mother had insisted they buy Lucy her own tent.

Scratch that.

Suddenly she wished her mother had insisted they all sleep in the same old tent they'd always used. What she wouldn't give to be quivering in her parents' arms, rather than holding her breath all alone. In the dark. With a monster on the other side of a very thin piece of blood red nylon.

"Get out of here! Go on!"

Her father's voice came loud and strong just a few feet away.

Pots clanged together, and the monster outside scurried off. She heard it breaking through the underbrush surrounding their campsite, and she breathed a sigh of relief.

"Lucy, are you—" Her mother broke off. "Go on! Go away! Shoo!"

The underbrush thrashed louder and louder until her mother screamed in fear. No, terror. The animal snarled and snapped its teeth. Her father shouted in alarm and then pain. Lucy sat frozen at the entrance of her tent, listening helplessly as the beast attacked her parents. Screams, growls, fabric shredding, dirt flying, bones crunching, and then silence.

Not silence. Only her parents were silent. The animal continued snarling and grunting and snuffling wetly as it did unspeakable things to the only people in the world she truly loved. A screech bubbled up her throat and it was all Lucy could do to keep her mouth clamped shut. But a tiny squeak managed to leak out.

And the animal went quiet.

Giant paws padded toward her tent.

Lucy remained still.

Then her tent exploded inward, razor sharp claws tearing through the fabric and slicing through her shoulder. Her screech finally flew free and she scrambled backward, away from all the sharp pointy things shredding the thin blood red nylon.

She screamed and screamed and screamed, and still the giant wolf tore apart her tent in a frenzy. Its claws raked down her leg and its fangs gnashed within an inch of her arm, but its body became entangled in the fabric. This only enraged it more. A bloodshot eye locked onto Lucy and she could have sworn the wolf smiled. But not a nice smile. A smile that said, "I can't wait to gobble you up, little girl!"

The cacophony was too much to hear anything beyond her own screams and those of the wolf, but the wolf heard something. It stopped moving. It turned its head, bloody drool dripping from its snout.

A howl. Close by. Then another.

The wolf growled, but not at Lucy. At least, not at first. It gave her a furious glare and then wriggled itself free from the remains of her tent and loped off into the forest.

"Jesus," Mason whispered when she finally stopped speaking. "What happened?"

Lucy shuddered, not wanting to remember *all* of what happened next. Mason wrapped his arm around her shoulders and held her trembling body close. She immediately felt calmer and leaned into him, taking comfort where she could find it.

"A hiker found us the next morning. I was in the hospital for two weeks. A bunch of people questioned me, told me everything would be okay. I guess they were right, in a way. By the time I went to recuperate at my grandmother's in Pepper, about an hour away from here, my college had been paid for, my parents' mortgage was paid off, and I had a healthy settlement from the Forest Service over the 'incident.' I still would have rather had my parents back."

They sat in silence for a moment, their ice creams forgotten and melting down their hands. She didn't care. Mason's closeness was all that mattered. He gave her strength she didn't know she possessed.

"I've spent the last ten years trying to build a life away from Ashtown, one that wasn't clogged with… memories. I went to school, I built a career as an accountant, I went to more therapists than Woody Allen. I put my past behind me."

"So, what brought you back to town? Selling the house?"

Heat bloomed in her cheeks. She'd already shared her deepest darkest secret with him. The latest bit of drama in her life barely compared.

"Long story short, I was framed for embezzling. Turns out that blood really is thicker than water. Especially, when the president of a family-owned company discovers his uncle has been feeding a bad gambling habit by stealing from the corporate bank account. After I tried reporting it to the authorities, the family covered the uncle's activities and pinned it on me. They couldn't press charges, of course, but they hid their tracks enough to satisfy the investigators. Then they took their revenge by spreading the word I was a thief. Good luck finding an accounting job with that kind of rumor going around."

"Assholes," Mason growled and then gripped his cone so tightly it crumbled in his hand.

Lucy smiled at his protectiveness. "Yeah, well, whaddya gonna do? My grandmother is great, but I needed to get away, go somewhere to regroup."

He threw his ice cream in the trash can next to the bench and shook off the droplets of creamy goodness before giving her a curious look. "You mean you needed someplace to hide."

A denial sprang to Lucy's lips, but before she could speak the words, she realized he was right. The truth hurt. She shrugged and tossed her own sloppy cone into the trash. For some strange reason, she'd lost her appetite.

Mason turned to her, took her sticky hand in his and gazed deeply into her eyes. "There's no reason to hide anymore, Lucy. I won't let you. You're too spectacular to hide away."

Tears burned at the backs of her eyes, but she couldn't look away from his hypnotizing green eyes. Not that she really wanted to.

"And you need to know," he continued, wiping a fleck of ice cream from her chin, "you'll never be alone again. You will *always* have me. Me, my brothers, my entire pack.

Your pack. You are the alpha mate, and every member of the pack will support you, no matter what."

Wouldn't that be nice? she thought. She wanted to believe him, more than anything. But life had a nasty way of reminding her that whatever progress she made, it would be there to take it all away.

"I don't know, Mason," she whispered, leaning her head on his shoulder.

He kissed her temple. "What don't you know, my love?"

"I'm not strong enough to take on that kind of responsibility. An alpha mate should be strong, a formidable force. That's just not me."

She felt his lips smile against her skin, and then he said, "You're wrong, but that's okay. I can be strong for the both of us until you realize it."

CHAPTER SIXTEEN

MASON AND LUCY SPENT THE REST OF THE AFTERNOON window shopping along the main drag. He'd expended a lot of effort building up Ashtown's reputation as the hottest spot for hipsters to hang, and it had worked. After they invariably moved on to fresher roadkill, the middle class would catch wind of the town's charms and it would be come all the rage with suburbanites. Then they would follow the hipsters' breadcrumbs, leaving Ashtown to the snowbirds. Then he'd just figure out how to repeat the cycle.

In the meantime, Lucy seemed to be having a great time pawing through all the junk that reminded her of her childhood. It warmed his heart to see his mate's spirits lift. She'd suffered enough in her life. It was time she enjoyed herself a little.

"I had this exact toy when I was nine," Mason said as he handed her a ninja action figure dressed in a red Hawaiian shirt. "It was my most prized birthday present that year. Then Kade stepped on it with his baseball cleats. Smashed it into a million pieces."

"I hope he replaced it for you with his allowance." She had a glint in her eye that suggested she already knew the Blackwood brothers weren't sitcom perfect. He laughed.

"Not a chance in hell. I was so mad I shifted and tackled him. Dad caught us before Kade got to shift, and I was grounded for a week. On my birthday!"

"Poor baby," Lucy mocked, stroking his arm like he was a whining puppy. "Stories like that make me grateful I was an only child."

"You never wanted someone to fight with? To share your clothes with? To tell your darkest secrets to?"

"Not really. Besides, I had my mom for fighting. At least during my teenage years." Mothers and daughters, an eternal struggle.

"So, you were a daddy's girl?"

Lucy snorted softly and played with the arm of an old Fisher Price record player. "No doubt about it. We loved to listen to his old Sinatra albums. I didn't really care so much about Ol' Blue Eyes, but I loved how much *he* loved him."

"We should go listen to some of them," Mason suggested, hoping she'd take the hint and invite him over to her house. Not that mates required invitations, but he was still trying to be a gentleman—at least until she finally accepted him as her mate.

Lucy sighed sadly. "Can't. I have his old record player somewhere, but the albums were stored in the basement and it flooded a few years back. The caretaker threw them all out. All I have left are the memories."

Mason grabbed her hand and dragged her from the little curio shop. "We can fix that."

As the Record Turns was one of the first "cool" shops to open on Main Street in recent years. He had no reason to visit the store often, but if someone was in the market for vintage vinyl, there was no better place in all of Georgia.

"Any one in particular?" he asked as he headed straight for a section at the back devoted to the Rat Pack.

"No idea. He had a bunch."

Mason felt the heat from Lucy's body as she peered over his shoulder while he flicked through the albums. His wolf urged him to pick her up, set her on the racks of records, and take her right there in the middle of *As the Record Turns*. The cashier, a mangy-looking dude with tiny braids in his beard and an unlit clove cigarette dangling from his tobacco-stained lips, probably would have enjoyed the show, but Mason *definitely* wasn't into other people watching. Especially Lucy. Even a brief glance from another man sent his wolf into a fit of jealousy. So, he kept his cool and continued digging.

"Will this do?" He showed her one titled *Frank Sinatra's Greatest Hits.* The man himself graced the cover with a cocky little smile Mason admired.

"Does it have *Fly Me to the Moon?*"

"Huh, I would have pegged you as a *My Way* kinda gal."

She nudged him with her hip, sending spirals of desire straight to his cock. "Ha-ha. I'm actually partial to *Moon River.*"

"How apropos." When she looked at him blankly, he sighed. "*Moon River?* Werewolf? Get it?"

"Oh God," she groaned.

What he wouldn't give to hear her moaning those words in his ear as he brought her to the edge of oblivion, over and over and over again. He pushed the image from his mind, but it was too late. His cock pressed hard and hot against the fly of his jeans.

"So what's yours?" she asked.

Mason was so distracted by her soft curves grazing his side as she read the list of songs including on the album that he had no clue what she was talking about. "Huh?"

"Your favorite Sinatra song."

"Oh. Sorry, I'm more of a Dean Martin guy."

Lucy gasped and slapped a hand to her chest. If she'd been wearing pearls, he had no doubt she would have clutched them for dramatic effect. "Say it isn't so!"

"Hey, your dad loved Sinatra. My mom was *in love* with Dino."

"Mama's boy," she teased.

He grinned as he pulled a Dean Martin LP from the rack. "Guilty as charged. I guess we'll just have to go back to your place and compare. My treat."

"Oh, I didn't know you were a glutton for punishment."

He waggled an eyebrow at her. "You have no idea."

Lucy blushed furiously and hurried out the door while he paid for the albums. He threw money at the kid behind the register and jogged after her, not wanting to let her out of his sight for a minute. He caught up with her as she entered the curio store again.

"What's up?" He fell in step next to her.

"Since you bought that for me, it only seems fair that I buy your little ninja dude."

"His name was Master Fu, and I don't need a toy."

"I don't need a record," she shot back.

"So that's how it's going to be, huh? Arguing over every

little thing for the rest of our lives?" He chuckled, but Lucy didn't.

She paled and turned away to the pay for Master Fu. Mason tried not to feel disappointed over her reticence to admit they were mates. His brain knew she'd come to eventually, and probably very soon. But in that moment, it still felt like a kick in the nuts.

The tension between them on the drive to her place drove Mason mad. He'd never felt so unsure in his life—an uncommon and extremely unwelcome feeling for an alpha. He vowed to let her take the lead, so when he pulled up in front of her place and she jumped out, he hesitated. Only when she glanced over her shoulder and said, "Coming?" did he follow.

By the time he closed her door—he'd had one of his men fix her broken doorknob—she was on the phone with the local pizza place. She gave him a quizzical look.

"Preferences?"

He shrugged.

"Okay," she said into the phone, "make it a large Hawaiian. Thanks. It'll be here in twenty minutes."

"You could have warned me you were planning to ruin a perfectly good pizza with pineapple."

"Hey, I asked," she said, leaning against the kitchen entryway, the picture of health and sass. "If you don't like the best pizza man ever invented, the door's right there."

"I'm not leaving until you admit I'm right."

Mason looked around the living room until he spotted the record player. It was old, but of high quality. Real audiophile equipment that must have set Lucy's father back quite a bit when he bought it. Lucy winced at the static crackling through the speakers as the needle skimmed over the old vinyl.

"I think I already won."

Then the music started, and Mason turned to her with his hand held out. "Care to dance?"

"No way, I'm a terrible dancer."

"I don't believe it."

She stepped away from the wall. Just a step, but it was a start. "I swear. One guy at a school dance asked if I had a bug crawling around under my shirt."

Mason laughed. "Now I *need* to see you dance!"

He breached the distance between them and clasped one of her hands. It was soft and warm and full of life. "Don't worry, I'm an excellent dancer."

"Cocky as ever," Lucy groaned, but she allowed him to pull her into his arms.

Her lush curves pressed into his chest, his stomach, his pelvis, his legs, driving his wolf wild. Driving *him* wild. His hands itched to skim those tempting peaks and valleys. Instead, he ground his teeth tight and simply

151

swayed with her in his arms. She kept her hands on his shoulders, as if they were at a chaperoned middle school dance.

"It would be easier if you wrapped your arms around my neck," he suggested coyly. The look in her eye told him he wasn't fooling anyone, which he really hadn't intended to.

"It would be easier if we were listening to Sinatra," she countered, but she wound her arms around his neck anyway.

They swayed together in the middle of the room until the first side of the record ended. The player had a special feature that allowed it to automatically flip over the album and start the next side without human intervention. They continued swaying through the process, heedless of the fact the player made a hell of a racket doing its job. They were too engrossed in their own closeness to care about anything else.

Until the doorbell rang.

"Pizza!" Lucy cried, pulling free from his hold and leaving him utterly and painfully alone.

He knew she wanted him, he could have smelled her desire a mile away. Yet she denied herself. He didn't really understand it, but she'd gone through so much in such a short period of time. *Take a deep breath*, he reminded his wolf, as much as himself. They'd promised to give her space. Taking a deep breath, he adjusted the crotch of his pants and sat on the couch.

Lucy returned with a slice of pizza dangling from her mouth. Her eyes rolled back in her head as she tossed the box at him and kicked back next to him, crossing her feet in his lap.

"Oh God, does everything taste so good when you're a wolf?"

She moaned with delight. Mason never in his life imagined he'd be jealous of a slice of pizza.

"No idea. I've always been a wolf. But I suspect your change is progressing, so you probably have heightened senses."

In less time than it took for the pizza to arrive, they'd devoured the entire pie—mostly Lucy. Her transformation was clearly using up a lot of calories, making her ravenous. Mason only hoped she'd be hungry for more than food. And soon.

"I don't think I've ever eaten half a pizza before," Lucy said as she stuffed their grease-soaked napkins in the empty box.

"Half?" Mason challenged.

She laughed and then stood, moving toward the door. "Thank you for a lovely day, Mason. I can't believe I'm saying this, but I had a lot of fun."

Mason stood too, but he didn't acknowledge her moon-sized hint. Instead he headed for the stairs. "I did too, Lucy. And now it's time for bed."

Ignoring her stuttering and huffing, he headed directly to her room, using his sense of smell to track it down. It probably looked exactly as it did the day her parents died —posters of old boy bands, a few vestiges of her obvious 'pretty, pretty princess' stage, and a closet full of outdated clothing.

"What do you think you're doing?"

He eyeballed her narrow queen-sized bed. "You need a bigger bed."

"It's plenty big," she argued. Always arguing!

"For you. But you have a mate now. A big one."

Her growl of irritation—mixed with the scent of her sudden surge of desire—made his dick harder than he could ever remember it being. She really was quite a specimen! He smiled and stepped up close to her, gathering her in his arms. Her eyes grew wide when he pressed his cock against her hip and her breathing grew shallow.

Leaning in, he whispered in her ear. "If I leave, will you come with me?"

She shuddered. "No," she breathed.

"And that's why I'm staying here tonight. You're my mate, and you might find this hard to believe, but I can't bear to be apart from you."

She pulled back and stared up at him, her breath coming in hot, short bursts. Her growing need swirled and mixed with his own. She was utterly perfect. Utterly *his*.

CHAPTER SEVENTEEN

Lucy swallowed hard, mouth suddenly dry. She couldn't bear to be apart from him either. Not when she felt his desire like a hot brand against her hip. Not when the musky scent of his desire teased her nose.

Coarse, callused fingers brushed her skin as he nimbly unfasted one button after another. The balsam and clove and pure sex smell of him embraced her in a deliciously wicked hug. His warmth sank into her, heating her from outside in, fanning the flames of her own arousal. It made her ache and her pussy throb, her body desperate for his touch.

It was almost more than she could bear. To have a man this gorgeous—this masculine, attentive, and powerful—drinking her in like she was the sweetest dessert... It made her want all the more.

She'd been with men in the past—boyfriends who'd claimed to love her and the odd one-night stand—but she'd never felt like *this*. None of them touched her—looked at her—as if they craved her more than air in their lungs. Or looked at her like she was so precious she should be worshiped and admired.

It felt so good and yet was so very, very bad. She couldn't allow herself to fall into his trap. Whatever Mason said about mates, she couldn't get used to this feeling of being desired, craved. Like she was something to be savored and cherished. As if she had value beyond measure.

Because when he was gone? She didn't think she could ever find someone who made her feel so much ever again. He was a one in a million type of man. Someone to be trusted. Someone she could... love.

With that thought came the urge to pull away. The need to tell him it was all too much. It poked and prodded her to save her heart. Run. Hide. But then she lifted her gaze to his and it all... fell away. Those terrible doubts fell away as she fell into a molten puddle in his arms.

Mason lowered his head, toned, firm lips scorching her skin as he caressed her lips and then teased the line of her jaw. He continued, mouth dancing over her skin until he reached the space right below her ear. A tremble of desire slithered through her with that touch, a zing of arousal spearing her.

His talented fingers brushed the underside of her bra,

calluses scraping the delicate silk and lace. Lucy sighed and leaned into him, needing to feel the hard planes of his body against her curves. His hand delved beneath the fabric of her bra, pads of his fingers ghosting over the stiff peak of her sensitive nipple.

Lucy rolled her shoulders, allowing her shirt to slide down her arms and fall to the floor. Mason didn't hesitate to take advantage of the added room, his free hand sliding to her back. A quick twist undid the clasp of her bra and then that too tumbled to the ground. Those teasing, scorching kisses paused just long enough for him to draw back to stare down at what he'd just revealed.

She followed his line of sight, a sliver of self-consciousness easing into her blood for a moment—her soft stomach and large breasts nothing like the toned women of the pack. But he merely licked his lips, eyes brightening to amber, and pulled his lips back in a wicked smile.

Mason massaged her breast, cupping the fullness and rubbing his thumb back and forth across her hardened nipple. He scraped the firm nub with his thumbnail and she shivered with his touch.

"You're even more gorgeous than I imagined." His lips ghosted over the shell of her ear. "And I imagined *a lot.*"

Lucy grinned and turned her head, lips tingling with the need to taste him—explore every inch of his body. Only to have him nudge her away.

"Not tonight. Tonight I'm going to make *you* happy. Very, *very* happy." As if to prove his point, his touch went to her shorts and he quickly unbuttoned them before lowering the fly.

"I guess you have experience taking shorts off me," she teased.

"I do." He flashed her a grin. "But this time I get to look." Without another word, he dropped to his knees and tugged on her shorts. The fabric clung to her hips for a moment before sliding down her thighs and falling into a heap at her feet.

Mason's breath caught, his attention wholly on Lucy's pussy. Or rather, the sheer white panties that barely shielded her from his gaze.

"Lucy," he whispered her name ever so softly. "Did you dress up for me?" He glanced at her but before she could form a snappy comeback, his mouth was on her skin. He teased her inner thighs, nudging her gently so she would spread her legs for him.

Mason lapped at her skin—soft, gentle licks over her warming flesh as he ventured north. She shivered with every searing kiss, every tormenting caress of his tongue on her body. Her nipples hardened even further, the need surging through her like a punishing wave of desire.

Why had she said she couldn't mate him, again? Whatever her reasons, they seemed insignificant now. Like nothing in the face of the devastating pleasure Mason could cause.

And fuck, she knew it'd be good. So very, very good. There was no way this man wouldn't make her scream his name while she forgot her own.

She opened her mouth to... what? Beg? Plead? Promise damn near anything if he'd just *touch* her already? And then... then he did. His strong hands rose to tease the hem of her panties, talented digits dipping beneath the elastic to torment her sensitive skin.

"Mason," she whispered. A soft plea for more.

He silently denied her, mouth dipping low once more as he ignored where she needed him most. He returned to the inside of her thighs, teasing them with the same fierce determination he'd shown before.

It'd turned into torture now. To watch him, over six feet of hardened muscle and sexy man fully dressed as he kissed her. As he edged nearer and nearer to her aching pussy. She at least wanted to rip his clothing from his body, watch his rippling muscles as he gripped her thighs. Watch his thick cock surging into her wet sheath, claiming her with his body.

She wet her lips and other imaginings filled her mind. The thought of taking him into her mouth rising above all others. She'd lick him slowly, lap at the salty liquid on the tip of his cock before taking him deep once more. Slow and steady at first, then taking more, moving faster and faster until his knees went weak and he begged for mercy.

She smiled with those wicked thoughts, her core pulsing

and clit twitching with the erotic imaginings. Only to have the day dream wiped from existence when his talented lips found the hem of her panties once more. Not just lips. His tongue traced the edge of lace and she shuddered with the promise of pleasure.

"Mason," she panted and moaned, that tongue giving her a promise of more, but not quite yet.

Except this time he seemed to understand, seemed to know that he'd pushed her to the edge of her control. Mason's mouth abandoned her but only for a moment. Just long enough for deft fingers to take the place of his tongue. For him to tug the scrap of silk and lace aside and bare her wet pussy to the room's cool air. He exposed her wet, needy flesh, body trembling in anticipation of what was to come. He pursed his lips and leaned forward, brushing a soft, sweet, and all too brief kiss across her sex lips. And no matter how chaste the kiss, that single caress lit the flames of her desire more than any man in her past.

She couldn't wait for him to finally take her into his arms. To wrap around her and consume her with his desire until she fainted from the pleasure. Hell, she'd probably die.

Mason hooked his thumbs beneath the waist of her panties and gave a gentle tug, the silk tracing her hips before they tumbled to the ground. A raw, carnal growl vibrated through the air, rumbles sinking into her and forcing her desire to climb even higher.

"Absolutely fucking perfect," he breathed deeply and

groaned. "I can't wait to spread your thighs and see every last inch of you."

"But not before I get a chance to unwrap you." Her voice was more coarse and needy than she'd ever heard it before.

Mason pushed to his feet in a single fluid move, his gaze never leaving hers. She sensed his indecision combating his desire and all-consuming hunger, and he finally shook his head—denying her.

"Not yet." He shook his head.

"But I want…"

"I know what you want." He reached up and back, grabbing his shirt between his shoulder blades, and tugged, whipping the fabric over his head. "But tonight, this is all you get."

Lucy drank him in, studying the chiseled contour of his pecs, abs, and even bulky triceps. He was more Greek god than human and she wondered if it was too late to change her mind. Too late to beg for all of him.

"Get back on the bed." Mason's voice was all grit and gravel. "Open those pretty thighs for me and if you're a good girl, I'll take off the rest."

Lucy swallowed hard and then moved faster than she ever had in her life.

ONCE HE HAD LUCY ON THE BED BEFORE HIM, BODY BARED to his gaze, his mind raced with every fantasy he could conjure. Still, before he moved, he gave himself a moment to savor the sight of her—savor the blessing he'd received.

Because fuck if she wasn't a blessing from God.

Her soft, creamy thighs were spread, revealing the pale pink sweetness that waited for him. Her pussy lips were flushed with arousal, that intimate part of her slick with proof of her desire. Even in the dim light of the room, he could see the glistening wetness on her folds. His mouth watered and he licked his lips, imagining the musky sweetness of her feminine cream as it slid over his taste buds.

Mason reached down and palmed his cock, giving himself a harsh squeeze to try and temper the harsh edge of his need. He ached to free himself, to sink into her over and over again until there was no telling their bodies apart.

He leaned down and prowled onto the bed, climbing between her thighs like a wolf on the hunt for sensual prey. In truth, he was a beast searching out a meal to sate his need. What the beast craved, it caught, and his next meal was laid out before him. He reached for her silken thighs, hands grasping her plump, soft flesh. He massaged her gently, taking his time to stare at Lucy, his gaze raking over the soft curve of her exposed breasts and pebbled nipples.

How many times had he imagined this moment? Having

his mate splayed in front of him, ready and willing? Probably too many to count, and still his fantasies paled in comparison to the woman in front of him now.

"Mason," she whined. "You're driving me crazy."

He wanted to laugh. Her desperation could only be a fraction of his own. The pounding of his heart, the answering throb of his cock, was nearly too much to bear. Still, he held his breath and reminded himself that tonight was for Lucy.

Tonight, she'd know ecstasy in a way she could never have imagined. His fangs descended at the thought and he growled low to himself, a reminder to keep his wolf in check. There would be time for more—for everything —later.

With one final glance at her incredible body, he lowered himself to the bed, lying between her spread thighs. He moved to his left first, kissing his way up her leg, pausing to lap at her skin and savor those sweet flavors. He eased higher, drawing nearer to that space he was drawn to, but he forced himself to turn to his right instead. He repeated the process, licking and nuzzling her flushed skin, breathing deeply and memorizing the intricate scent of her arousal.

With every lick, the scent of her desire clouded the air more and more. It intoxicated him, begging him without words to find her core and lap up every droplet of her cream.

She arched and writhed at his touch, twisting her hips and moving her body as if to force him to move where she needed him. She whimpered and whined as he traveled along her thighs, reaching the crease where her leg met her hips. So close to her pussy, right at that delicate skin. He nuzzled her, breathing deeply and savoring her musky scent.

His cock throbbed in his pants, the pulsing ache matching his heartbeat and sending a thumping need scorching through his veins. His balls were heavy between his legs, filled with cum he ached to spill into Lucy. Fill her with his scent, claim her with his body in every way possible.

But not yet. Soon, but not yet.

For now, he'd cherish everything she gave him. He turned his head, moving that last inch until her closely cropped curls teased the tip of his nose. Her wet slit was there and he couldn't hold himself back any longer. He lapped at her soft, sweet core, gathering every hint of her salty-sweet musk. He tasted her hot, wet need, and she bucked against his lips.

"Mason," she breathed out with a long sigh, but his next move turned that into a deep moan. He found her clit—that aching bundle of nerves swollen against his lips—and he circled the hard nub with his tongue. He flicked the small bit of flesh, movement hummingbird fast as he drove her pleasure higher and higher. She gripped the sheets, tugging and pulling on them with her white-knuckled grip.

He hummed, circling her over and over until she moved her hips in time with his mouth, silently willing him not to stop. She craved more and he wanted to be the one to give her all she desired.

Just not yet.

Mason eased away from her clit, giving it a last, sensuous lick before moving on to explore her feminine folds.

"I need," she panted. "I need, I need…"

He knew what she needed as if they were one. He eased two fingers inside her slick channel, closing his eyes as her inner walls quaked around him. She ground into his touch, seeking out additional pleasure. He withdrew and pushed inside her once more, savoring her every moan and cry. He allowed a rumbling growl to come forward and flicked his tongue out to slowly circle her throbbing clit. The vibrations traveling into her, Lucy cried out with a soft gasp and a sharp yell.

"That's it," he paused to murmur. "Show me how much you like it."

And she did. She rode his hand like she couldn't get enough, like she couldn't live without his touch. He imagined what she'd do to his cock when he finally shoved himself inside her. Harder and faster, she worked his fingers while he licked and teased her clit. He met her stroke for stroke as the rolling of her hips became desperate and frenzied.

It took everything in him not to tear his pants from his body, grip his cock, and jerk his dick in time with her every movement. He wouldn't claim her—wouldn't violate her trust—but fuck his body ached. But there was no time to do anything. Lucy hovered on the brink, her body trembling as she approached release.

Mason curled his fingers, teasing that spot inside her sheath, while he gave her clit one long lick and then sucked hard on the sensitive button. Lucy screamed long and loud, his name on her lips while she slammed her hands against the bed. She whimpered as her walls shuddered and quaked around his fingers, so hard and fast he thought she might break them.

"That's it, baby." He slowed his attentions, easing her back to earth until the final shudders attacking her subsided. He eased his fingers free of her tight embrace and lifted his gaze to find her smiling at the ceiling. Eyes closed, skin glowing, her breaths came in long, slow pants.

"Oh my God," she whispered.

Mason grinned, loving that look on her face, and chuckled.

"Oh shit." Her breath escaped in a long huff. "That was..." She lifted her head, one eye opening slightly. "Give me a minute and I'm all about returning the favor."

He chuckled. "Not tonight, baby. This was all about you. Now it's time to get some rest."

"But…"

Aw, fuck. She pouted with her plump lower lip pushed out, and he damn near caved. His wolf wanted him to give in—to take the pleasure she offered and get closer to their mate. His dick… it was all on board with feeling her small hand wrapped around his shaft.

Except he hadn't been lying. Now wasn't the time. His sweet mate needed rest. And, as she continued to tempt him with that sweet pout, he crawled up beside her and snuggled her close.

CHAPTER EIGHTEEN

Lucy woke with a jolt. Her dreams of running through the forest as a wolf, Mason at her side, lingering. Their presence left her confused, wondering where she was. She blinked hard and recognized her childhood bedroom. She was home. Relief set in, but it evaporated on her next breath.

Smoke.

Squinting toward the open bedroom door—hadn't they closed it?—she spied clouds of smoke billowing up the stairwell and filling the landing. She coughed and reached for Mason. They needed to get out of there immediately.

But his side of the bed was empty. Warm, but empty.

"Mason?"

A hulking shadow shifted in the far corner of her room.

She barely caught the movement, but she instantly knew it wasn't a human.

"Mason?" she asked again, her voice shaking as hard as the rest of her body.

Something was wrong. Mason would have answered her by now. In fact, he would have woken her at the first whiff of smoke. He certainly wouldn't have let her call out for him without somehow comforting her. Even in his wolf form. She knew that deep in her heart.

The landing glowed from the fire downstairs. The shadow moved closer, amber eyes catching the light. Her heart thudded. Those weren't Mason's eyes. She'd only seen him in his wolf form once, but his eyes had remained green.

Not amber.

A deep growl reverberated through the room, setting every hair on her body on end. Something raged and whimpered inside her. Her mysterious wolf, possibly? Was she finally getting ready to become a full-fledged werewolf? Just as some mad creature was about to have her for a juicy midnight snack? The shadow took another menacing step.

Lucy froze, petrified.

Then the room exploded in a frenzy of fur and snarls. Lucy curled up into a ball, waiting for the fangs to sink deep into her flesh and tear her apart, just as they had her parents. Mason had abandoned her to the depraved torture of this lunatic, rogue wolf—whoever he was.

Glass shattered. Then the sound of bodies hitting the ground reached her disbelieving ears. Bodies. Plural. Somehow her new wolfy-senses allowed her to know without a doubt that *two* bodies had just hit the ground a full story down.

Lucy scrambled across the bed and peered out the demolished window. Two wolves lay on the ground below, stunned from the fall. But both stirred. One was light brown, the other was as black as the night. Mason. She'd recognize him anywhere.

He was first on his feet, but not by much. Just as he was about to clamp impossibly long canines into the other wolf's throat, it jerked sideways and clamped down on Mason's shoulder. From her vantage point, Lucy didn't hear Mason make a noise, but somewhere inside she felt his pain. It was intense and burning and primal.

Before she understood what was happening, her own canines grew a good two inches, protruding from her lips. She explored the sharp tips with her fingers, marveling at the change for a brief flash, before she was overcome by the need to rip out the throat of the asshole who had just hurt her mate.

Lucy sprinted from the room, naked as the day she was born, and took the stairs two at a time, never coming remotely close to losing her footing. As a full human, she could never have managed the feat, but more of her inner wolf was revealing itself, and she liked it. At the base of the stairs, she paused, trying to locate the source of the fire. She relaxed, letting the essence of her wolf take over and sniff it out.

Kitchen.

Good, that meant the back door would hopefully be safe. Sprinting for the back of the house, she discovered that whoever that asshole was, he'd set fires in multiple locations around the house. The back door was fully engulfed.

Lucy darted into her father's den, which had sat dusty and unused for a decade but was now filled with acrid smoke that choked her. No flames...yet. Throwing open a window, she crawled through the space and tumbled to the ground, her feet getting tangled up in a hoe the gardener must have left behind. Where was her inner wolf when she needed it?

Mason and the arsonist were locked in battle in her backyard. Gnashing teeth, slashing claws, guttural snarls. They writhed around on the ground, their bodies twisting and changing position so quickly she could barely keep track of who was who.

Out of the corner of her eyes, she spotted two wolves who looked familiar. Mason's guards. They stood at attention, the fur along their spines standing on end, but neither moved. Lucy looked between them, disbelieving.

"Do something!" she screamed at them.

They glanced in her direction and then a quiet voice reached out to her through the smoky air.

"When one alpha challenges another, it's forbidden for anyone else to join the fray."

"Are you fucking kidding me?" she screeched at them, but they kept their focus on the fight.

Mason yelped and limped away from the strange wolf, putting distance between them. The other wolf howled in triumph. Prematurely, as it turned out, when Mason tackled him. Hard.

Lucy snarled with approval. Her wolf side was growing stronger, more assertive, but something tickled the back of her human brain. Something familiar. The wolf. That howl. Then his eyes latched on to her and her world spun on its axis.

She was transported back to the forest, back to that terrible night ten years earlier. The moonlight shimmering through the trees, the unmistakable sound of claws digging at the earth, the grunts, the yelps, the growls. The blood, the pain, the anguish.

"He was there," she whispered.

She knew it down to her very cells. That wolf had been there the night her parents died. He wasn't the one to do the killing—that wolf had been a darker brown, with deep brown, very bloodshot eyes—but he hadn't stopped it.

He'd howled at some point. That's all Lucy knew. And it was exactly the same. Not just any howl, but one of achievement, of pride.

That night, Lucy's entire life had changed. She'd lost everything she cared about. And now the same dickwad was back, trying to ruin her life again!

"Not on my watch," she growled, ignoring the heat against her back as her house burned.

The house didn't matter anymore. She could live without her father's old golf clubs or her mother's hand-crocheted afghans. She could even live without the family photo albums. She couldn't live without her mate.

Recalling how easily her wolfy senses had come forward when she'd relaxed a little, Lucy focused on calming her mind. As much as she wanted to, she still couldn't shift into wolf form, but the beast was lurking just under the surface, giving her strength and courage she'd never before felt.

Snatching up the hoe, Lucy strode straight up to the fighting pair of wolves, despite the silent warnings from the guards. They could stand around like pussies if they wanted, but she wasn't about to let some antiquated form of machoism keep her from protecting her mate. Mason would do the same for her, and if he didn't like it, too freaking bad.

Hefting the hoe like a baseball bat, Lucy waited for a clear shot at the mad wolf's head. Her hands twitched with a need to bash his head in. With each passing second and every brutal swipe of his claws, her rage grew. It grew until it burned hotter than her house. Hotter than the sun.

Almost like clouds opening up to reveal a ray of sunlight, the many moving body parts stilled for the briefest moment. Just long enough for her to have a perfect view of the wolf's head. Lucy didn't hesitate. Leading with her hips—just as her father had taught her so many years earlier—she poured every ounce of energy and pain and love and hate into that swing.

CRACK!

The blunt end of the hoe bounced off the wolf's skull, sending the beast flying backward. Mason whipped his head around, seeking out the source of the mysterious attack on his foe. He tried to reach her mind, but she shut down the connection and advanced on the dazed stranger.

But not a stranger. Not really. He was there. He could have stopped it.

Lifting the hoe over her head, she brought the blunt end down on his head again with a satisfying *THWAP*.

"How *dare* you do nothing to save my parents!"

THWAP!

"How *dare* you set fire to my home!"

THWAP!

"How *dare* you attack my mate!"

The creature had stilled, but she could still feel it's cold, black heart beating weakly. Not for long. Spinning the hoe in her hands, Lucy took a deep breath and mustered every ounce of strength her own wolf could give her.

"HOW MOTHER FUCKING DARE YOU!"

The blade of the hoe buried itself deeply into the temple of the wolf, and the thing finally lay perfectly still. She struggled to yank the hoe free, wanting to continue pummeling the beast, desperate to keep hurting him until she was free from the pain deep inside her. Then strong arms wrapped around her and pulled her back. She struggled against them, but Mason's voice calmed her instantly.

"Shh, Lucy. It's over now."

Her entire body started shaking uncontrollably as she stared down at the mess she'd made. She wasn't happy to have taken a life, but she didn't regret it. Whoever this was, he'd deserved to die. It was still a shock to her system.

"He was there," she whispered, turning to bury her face in Mason's chest. "He was there! He watched as that wolf killed my parents and then tried to kill me!"

She was babbling and she knew it. She barely understood her own words, so most likely Mason couldn't, but somehow he knew. The connection between them was strong, so he knew. Still, she had to speak the words.

"He knew."

"Shh, he can't hurt you anymore, Lucy."

Pulling her face from the comfort of his bare chest, Lucy sought out his gaze. "I feel like I'm losing my mind, Mason. I feel... lost."

His lips twitched upward into a gentle smile. "Never, my love. You'll never be lost. I will always find you."

CHAPTER NINETEEN

Lucy refused to leave her family home until it was reduced to a pile of soggy, smoking rubble. One of Mason's sentries had retrieved two sets of baggy sweatsuits to cover their human forms before the first fire engine arrived, and the sentries had dragged the dead wolf deep into the woods, where it would rot into the earth in a matter of months.

Justice.

As they'd watched red and white lights dance in the dark trees, Mason held Lucy in his arms, doing his best to give her the comfort she needed. He'd tried talking her into returning to the pack house, but she'd simply shaken her head and stared as the roof had caved in. So he stood with her and would continue until she finally said goodbye to her past.

By the time the sky began to lighten with shades of lavender and apricot, the firefighters were packing up their engines and Lucy leaned all of her weight against him. She was still standing, but just barely. Bending low, he scooped her into his arms and carried her to the Cherokee. This time she didn't protest, just snuggled into his chest and passed out. She didn't even twitch when he settled her into the passenger's seat, or when he carried her into the pack house, or when he laid her in their bed and tucked her in.

Mason had pointedly ignored the National Circle, who'd all been waiting in the living room of the pack house when he'd returned, and he ignored their pointedly loud conversation just outside his door. He needed to rest as much as Lucy—much more than they needed an explanation of the night's events. Hopefully by the time he woke, the wounds he'd suffered in the fight would have healed a little, and he'd have the energy to give them the answers they needed. Pulling her body into his, Mason drifted off, only to have Lucy wake him thirty seconds later.

"Good morning," she murmured, resting her chin on his chest.

He yawned and stretched. "Hey, what time is it?"

"Ten."

"Ten?" Mason jerked upright in surprise.

Three hours had slipped by. He didn't care so much about

the NC, but Lucy needed answers and he wanted to be there when she was ready.

"He was there," she said quietly, her eyes pleading with Mason to help her make sense of it all.

"I know." He pulled her down with him and held her tightly.

"How? How could you know?"

"I didn't until last night, once you said so. Then it all made sense."

He stared at the swirls in the ceiling, trying to figure out the best way to tell her the whole story. She waited patiently, her fingers splayed across his chest.

"His name is—*was*—Frank Riverson. He was the alpha of the Riverson pack. They were our neighbors on the other side of the mountain. We coexisted peacefully for many generations. In fact, my brother Gavin and Frank's son, Brian, were best friends growing up."

Mason recalled the two pups wrestling like maniacs every time the Blackwoods met up with the Riversons. Jacob, the Blackwood alpha and Mason's father, would sit with Frank and watch the boys play while they discussed the politics of leading a wolf pack. But Frank's mate, Kathy... she'd always seemed a little off to Mason. As it turned out, for good reason.

"We didn't discover this until it was too late, but apparently it was an open secret within the Riverson pack that Kathy had been skirting the edge of becoming feral for some time. Everyone knew it, but because she was the alpha mate, they said nothing. Some claimed it wasn't their place—Frank should have been the one to eliminate the threat. But he didn't. Instead, he kept a close eye on her, so she didn't do anything crazy. Then one day she disappeared."

Lucy's skin pebbled under his hands. She knew what was coming, but she remained silent. Listening. Waiting.

"The pack searched for her, but Frank found her. By then, it was too late for your parents and Frank doesn't deserve any credit for your survival. Once my father discovered what had happened, he did his duty and dispatched the feral wolf so she couldn't hurt anyone else. Of course, not without a fight from Frank, Brian, and a handful of other Riverson wolves."

"What happened to them?"

"Those who protected Kathy were sent away by the National Circle and the pack was disbanded. Many joined our ranks, but some didn't. I got word last week that Frank had been rehabilitated and released. Some nonsense about how their fated mate bond had muddled his brain with her crazy, but he admitted the error of his ways and took full responsibility. I knew it was all bullshit, but you can't argue with the NC."

"So why did he attack now? Didn't your father pass away a few years ago?"

A jolt of grief surprised Mason. Losing his father had nearly broken him. He'd only survived through the support of the pack, and though it was difficult, he'd buried himself in his role as the new alpha, if only to honor his father.

"My best guess is that since my father is dead, he put the blame for his mate's death on me. He must have sniffed out that you were my mate and decided to go after you as payback."

Lucy rubbed a scar on her shoulder thoughtfully. "Or to finish what his mate started."

"One more thing you should know. My father arranged to pay your medical bills and set you up with a scholarship, funded by what remained in the Riverson coffers once the pack was disbanded, not the Forest Service. That was just his cover."

"That was kind of him," Lucy said quietly.

Mason pulled her tightly, closing his eyes and breathing in her scent. She smelled of bitter smoke and sadness, but he could also smell the wild musk of her wolf developing. Quickly. He hoped her transformation would be complete by nightfall. Then they could seal their bond in a more traditional—and immensely more pleasurable—way.

A soft knock rattled the door and pulled Mason out of the moment. The intruder was Kade, who poked his head into the room after Mason gave the all clear.

"Everyone wants to know how their alpha mate is doing," he said, smiling at Lucy. "And the NC are growing impatient. Roman said something about having better things to do than hang out in our living room for days on end."

"Fuck 'em," Mason growled, burying his face in Lucy's hair.

She stroked the back of his head. "No, we should go. I think we all need a little closure."

He might have been the Blackwood alpha, but he knew better than to argue with his mate when her mind was made up. She would be a strong alpha mate, one who could stand up to the most fearsome wolf in the pack and still expect him to rock her world afterword. What a woman!

The living room erupted with cheers and applause the moment Mason and Lucy rounded the corner. The place was packed to the rafters with Blackwood wolves, and they all wanted to welcome their new alpha mate. Lucy took it all in stride, returning hugs and kissing babies. She was in her element—a true alpha mate.

Three very large wolves hung back, watching the scene, biding their time. After the initial rush of handshakes, back slaps and congratulations, the men approached.

"Mason, we need to talk."

He couldn't put them off any longer. "Okay, Roman. Talk."

Roman's lips turned into a thin, hard line at how close Mason had come to insubordination, but he let it slide. It'd been a tough couple of days.

"We now believe your version of events. That Frank Riverson set the fire on your lands. That alone would be grounds for extermination." His gaze shot over to Lucy. "If your mate hadn't already handled the situation so skillfully."

"You heard?"

Roman nodded. "Your brothers filled us in. Frank was no longer an alpha, so her actions are considered self-defense instead of interfering with an alpha challenge. You should also know that we now have evidence linking the anonymous report of the illegal turning to Frank directly. It's clear to everyone that it was an accident, not intentional. As far as the National Ruling Circle is concerned, the matter is closed."

Mason huffed. "As it should have been from the start."

"*However,*" Roman continued, giving Mason a steely stare. "I think we can all agree that your pack's pups could certainly use some extra lessons in how to control themselves."

"Agreed," Mason said with a curt and slightly embarrassed nod. "Lucy will need the same training, so she can join the pups."

He glanced over at where she stood, holding a chubby

toddler. She tossed the girl in the air, a smooth-skinned child going up and a fluffy furball coming down. Lucy laughed and cuddled the wriggling pup before handing her back to her mother.

"She'll be an excellent alpha mate for your pack, Mason." Roman slapped Mason's back. "And good for you, too."

"I know. But that can't happen until *all* of the uninvited guests in this house get the hell out, so I can finally claim her."

Chuckling, Roman squeezed Mason's shoulder hard—one last demonstration of his position—before turning to leave. He almost tripped over a blurry figure darting between their legs and heading for Lucy.

"Miss Lucy!" Charlie Tipton shouted as he ran up to her, breathless and panting. "Ghosty... *pant pant* ...porch... *pant pant* ...burned... *pant pant* ...babies!"

CHAPTER TWENTY

"AREN'T THEY *CUTE*?" CHARLIE EXCLAIMED AS HE PEERED into the cardboard box sitting on the gigantic dining table in the middle of the pack house.

Lucy gently pulled him away to allow Drew room to examine the box full of kittens. The exhausted mama cat lay on her side, resting as her babies suckled. Her fur was grey, except where it was coated with soot.

"I still can't believe she managed to keep them all alive when the house literally burned down around them," she said, her fingers twitching to pick up a baby and give it sweet kisses. But she wasn't about to interrupt Drew's examination.

"It's a miracle," Robert Tipton said. "Charlie dragged me all the way over there, insisting we go save Ghost Kitty. I figured she'd have run off at the first whiff of smoke, but

186

she must have been in the process of giving birth, because there they were. Tucked up in the only remaining bit of house that hadn't burned to ash."

"You're a hero," Mason said, patting Charlie's back. The boy beamed up at his alpha.

Charlie wriggled out from under Lucy's hand and crawled onto the table to look at the kittens without getting in the way. "What should we name them?"

Lucy didn't want to get the boy's hopes up. "Why don't we wait to name them until Drew gives them a clean bill of health, okay?"

Drew gently laid the last kitten, this one black with tiny white mittens, against its mother's tummy and smiled. "No need to wait. Other than smelling like smoke, they're all fit as a fiddle. Now you just need to figure out what to do with them."

"Keep them," Lucy said.

"Get rid of them," Mason said at the same time.

Lucy gasped and shot him a dark look, daring him to say it again. Ghost Kitty had defied the odds and survived a fire that destroyed an entire house and a lifetime of memories. They were the last surviving memories of her family home, her parents. She'd fight Mason if she had to, but she had a feeling should could convince him.

Somehow.

"We're not keeping those cats," he said, squinting hard at her.

She ignored him and turned back to Charlie. "Well, Ghosty already has a name, so what about the rest?"

"That one has mittens, maybe we could call it...um..."

"Lucy, we're not keeping these cats," Mason growled. "They're puppy food. We're wolves. Wolves *do not* own cats."

Lucy gave him a defiant smirk. "You're absolutely right, my love. Cats do the owning."

"Lucy..."

Drew glanced between them nervously. "And that's my cue."

He was followed out of the house by Robert, who had to drag poor Charlie away from the kittens he still wanted to name. In the matter of a minute, the entire pack house echoed with emptiness. Only Lucy and Mason remained.

"Argue all you like," Mason said, crossing his bulging arms over his barrel chest with an air of finality, "but this is *my* house and *my* rules."

Lucy glared up at him, tingles of frustration and anticipation skittering across her skin. "In the human world, married couples .share ownership of all their belongings. Is it the same in wolf packs?"

He simply smirked, and one eyebrow shot up in challenge.

Lucy glanced into the box to make sure Ghosty and her babies were settled. Then she grabbed a fistful of Mason's smoky sweatshirt, pulling him along.

"Where are you taking me?" he said with a chuckle, as if he didn't know.

She shot him a smirk over her shoulder without losing a step. "Well, I have to claim my half of this house, don't I?"

Mason laughed, not fighting as she dragged him up the stairs to their bedroom.

With every step her heart pounded a hint faster, her blood racing through her veins and making her head swim. She drew in a lungful of air, catching the scent of his growing desire. It only thickened as they reached the hallway, and her own wanting swam in the air around them.

Lucy took a deep breath, willing herself to focus on the now, on every kiss, lick, and tease. On the hard plane of his muscles and the way he looked at her. He stared at her as if the entire world could burn down around them and he didn't give a damn.

But it wasn't enough for her. The small details, the things to be savored and cherished? Those were for another time. A time when her curiosity had long been satisfied. When she finally knew what waited for her in those tight, dark jeans of his. When she knew what it felt like to have him hard and deep inside her pussy.

Another handful of steps and they reached their

destination, bedroom door standing wide for them. She hauled him in and practically slammed the door shut before spinning to grab the hem of his shirt.

He laughed. "I can do it myself."

"Not a chance," she countered and yanked on the shirt, whipping it over his head. He flashed her a grin that had her panties growing even wetter and moved to help her with her own. Not happening. She shook her head.

"Hell no." She returned his grin. "You tortured me. It's my turn to return the favor." And she couldn't wait to unwrap her present.

She pressed to her tiptoes and sought his neck, kissing the cords of his throat while she rested her palms on the hard muscles of his tanned abs. She gripped his toned waist, letting the warmth of his body pour into her as she continued her travels. She kissed him lower, tongue flicking out to lap at his heated skin. Her lips teased his dusting of chest hair and then lower still, to his stomach and belly button. Which led to... that patch of hair that beckoned her to dip beneath the waistline of his jeans.

So close to his cock, his scent surrounded her, urging her to take more. To drink in his flavors and revel in the passion they could share. Her mouth watered and she settled on her knees as she reached for the button on his pants. She flicked the closure, fingers going to the zipper and dragging it down slowly. A low, oh-so-sexy growl slipped past his lips and she turned her attention to

Mason. Those eyes flickered amber, his beast dancing right on the edge of her mate's control. His hands remained fisted at his sides, white knuckles revealing how hard he fought to restrain himself.

She wanted to break that restraint.

She grinned, offering him a teasing smile, before she grasped his jeans and boxers both. With a tug she dragged them down his thighs, freeing his hard cock from its tight confines.

She licked her lips, eyeing the small droplet lingering on the tip of his dick. She could hardly tear her eyes away, entranced by his hardness. Mason was more than she could ever have imagined—thick, long, and so fucking hard for her. Her pussy clenched and her clit twitched, body preparing for his intimate possession.

But first, a taste...

She grasped his length, fingers wrapping around his hardness. Like silk over steel, he was warm against her palm, shaft throbbing in time with his pulse. She leaned forward, drawing in the air around them and memorizing his heated scent. She parted her lips, tongue creeping out to flick against the sensitive head of his cock. A sweet saltiness burst across her taste buds and she couldn't suppress the groan that flowed from her chest. A groan that Mason matched while his hips jerked.

"You're going to kill me," he rasped.

Lucy flashed him a wicked smirk and a wink. Then she focused on her task—driving Mason wild. She opened her mouth wide and took the head of his dick into her mouth, moaning with the explosion of flavors. She slid down his shaft and then back up again, taking him slow and deep before pulling away to press a soft kiss to the tip. "I can stop if you want."

"Not on your life," he growled then, his fingers going to her hair and fisting her strands. Holding her but not forcing her to move. No, he left the teasing up to her. She licked his shaft, tongue dancing over his length as she took him deeper and deeper still. She swallowed more of him—as much as she could—until he touched the back of her throat.

But it wasn't enough. There was still so much more of him.

She worked his length with her hand, palm gliding over his shaft while she teased his balls with her other hand. She moved up and down, humming in the hopes of sending the sweet vibration thrumming through his system.

And based on the way he gripped her hair harder and pulled her closer? He liked every bit of it.

"Fuck, Lucy," he ground out, his wolf adding a rumble to his words. "At least let me see you."

She smiled around his rigid cock and flicked her eyes at

him. Not releasing her prize, she gave a gentle shake of her head.

That rolling growl turned into a snarl, shocking her motionless.

"That's it," he snarled and gently tugged on her hair as he shifted his hips away from her mouth. He slipped past her lips with an audible pop and then encouraged her to stand. He kept up the pressure on her hair, forcing her to tip her head back and meet his stare. "I'm done waiting, Lucy. I want to fuck you so hard neither of us can move. I'm going to pound this sweet little pussy and coat you in my scent. And I'm gonna do it now. Do you understand me?"

She offered him a teasing smile, his rough tugs and erotic words arousing her even more. They made her want. Made her *need*. "I dunno. Can you be more specific?"

Mason released her hair and kicked off his jeans before taking a step toward her. And then another. And another. Her muscular alpha in all his naked glory. He crowded her with his bulky frame, steering her where he wanted her to go. "You want specifics?" His tone sent a shiver down her spine. "How about I rip off your clothes, pin you to the headboard, and then push my cock into that sweet, sweet pussy over and over again until you can't do anything but scream my name?"

Lucy's mouth went dry and her pussy clenched. "That's very specific."

And sounded so damn fun.

"Damn right it is. I haven't been able to think of anything but being inside you since I caught your scent. Now, are you going to be good or do I need to redden that sweet ass of yours?" Another step closer. "I'll bend you over that bed and paddle your ass until it's red and hot and then I'll fuck you deep."

It was very, very tempting to be very, very bad. She licked her lips, unable to decide between an erotic spanking and feeling Mason inside her as soon as possible.

He cupped her cheek and rubbed the pad of his thumb across her swollen lips. "I used to think this mouth wasn't good for anything but talking back."

"And now?"

"Now that I've seen these lips wrapped around my cock?" He growled. "There are no words for that, beautiful."

His strong fingers gripped the hem of her shirt and she lifted her arms as he pulled the top over her head. With another quick move, her bra fell to the floor, baring her breasts to the cool room. Not waiting for Mason, she unbuttoned her shorts and wriggled out of them, leaving her in nothing but her tiny purple panties.

And even those didn't last long. Not when he hooked his thumbs beneath the sides and snapped the thin bits of elastic and cloth. They fluttered to the ground, another casualty of their passion.

He cupped her center, heel of his hand pressed against her sex lips and teasing her clit. "Fuck, you're so wet. Coating my hand, beautiful."

He rubbed her gently, back and forth, giving her a hint of pleasure with that nearly chaste touch. But it wasn't enough. Not nearly. She mewled and shifted against him, needing more, but he didn't give an inch.

"I need to see this pretty pink pussy again."

A shudder of need raced through her veins, making her tremble. "It's yours."

MASON FIGURED HE'D BEEN AS STRONG AS ANYONE COULD expect when an alpha faced his naked, willing mate.

HE CUPPED THE BACK OF HER HEAD AND HELD HER STEADY as he lowered his head. He crushed his lips to hers, loving the warm and swollen feel. They were plump and sensitive from sucking his cock and fuck... she'd done it well. Almost too well.

Even after days of waiting, hoping, and dreaming of being with her... He'd never wanted her more than when she smiled up at him while she had his dick in her warm, yielding mouth.

Fuck, but he'd almost come right there.

But he wasn't about to ruin their claiming night by popping too early.

He was going to have her, claim her, and then do it all over again. He wanted everyone to know Lucy was fully and completely *his*.

He swept his tongue inside her mouth, swallowing her moan as they began their push and pull. The rhythmic dance they'd soon mimic with their bodies distracted her as he led her back, back, and back until her knees met the mattress. With one last nudge, he broke their kiss and watched her fall back onto the bed. Her tits bounced when she landed, hard nipples practically begging to be touched, to be sucked.

"Fuck, you're breathtaking." He took a moment to stare at the creamy hills and valleys of her body, amazed that she was his—that they'd spend the rest of their lives together.

He was one lucky fucker.

"Yeah?" She nibbled her lower lip. "Why don't you come show me how you feel?"

Mason wasn't a dumb wolf. He didn't need to be asked twice. He placed his knee on the bed and leaned toward her, crawling across the soft surface while she wiggled away. He followed her until she reached the center of the mattress and then eased between her pale thighs. He continued to ease forward, not stopping until he could reach her hands... and pin them to the headboard.

Gripping them hard enough to tell her he meant what he said, he stared her in the eyes. "Don't move 'em."

A wave of her arousal, the scent of her slick pussy, reached out for him. Oh, she liked the idea, but he waited for her nod before he got to work.

Mason began his teasing at the shell of her ear. He teased the delicate skin and then moved on, searching out every tormenting spot he could imagine. The hollow beneath her ear, of course. The long line of her throat and then where her neck met her shoulder. That was a wolf's most sensitive place—where his mating bite would go.

He licked and kissed a path down her chest, nibbling the hollow of her collarbone before he moved on. He moved on to the roundness of her full breasts. He cupped the mounds, pressing them together as he flicked one nipple and then the other with his tongue. He sucked on the pebbled peaks, taking turns as he moved from one to the other. He paused and blew a puff of cool air across her damp skin, smiling at her needy whine. He drew her into his mouth once more, scraping a fang across the nubbin, and suddenly he had two claw-tipped hands buried in his hair.

Mason released her nipple with a soft *pop*, the cherry tip urging him to return and tease her a little more, but not quite yet. "If you move your hands, I stop. Do you want me to stop?"

Her hands disappeared in an instant, returning to the headboard without hesitation. "Don't you dare."

"Consider yourself warned then, beautiful."

He released her breasts and moved lower, down her soft stomach until he reached the apex of her sex. He breathed deeply, drawing in the heady scent of her arousal. His mouth watered and what he wouldn't give to taste her again. To spend hours lapping at her pussy. But his impatient mate didn't seem to want his mouth on her cunt. No, when he nuzzled the soft curls covering her sex, she rolled her hips and released a low growl. One that surged straight to his aching cock.

"Need you, Mason. Claim me. Mate me. Just..." she whined. "I need you inside me."

"Yeah?" he whispered and took his time, wanting to tease her a little more. He dipped a finger between her silky folds and groaned at the heated wetness he found. So fucking wet. Her pussy was all hot and wanting, her slickness just begging for him to sink into it with his throbbing dick. "You ready for me?"

"Yes," she hissed and trembled.

Mason brought his wet finger to his mouth and licked her sweet cream off, taking his time and savoring every drop. Once he swallowed the last morsel, he pushed up to kneel on the bed between her legs. Dick bobbing between them, he wrapped his hands around her thighs and tugged her down the bed, pulling her against him and spreading her wide.

He gripped his dick, squeezing his shaft at the base to hold off his orgasm. Seeing that pretty pink pussy all flushed and wet for him... *damn.*

He eased forward and rubbed the tip of his shaft along her slit, shuddering with that initial touch. He rubbed the spongy head over her clit, smiling when she arched her back and put her tits on perfect display. So beautiful. So sensual.

He lowered his cock, easing down to tease her opening. Her core kissed the tip of his dick, as if silently begging him to sink inside her. He eased in an inch and then retreated, a shallow penetration that tormented them both. Just a little. Just enough to drive them mad with need.

Lucy whimpered. "Don't tease. Don't tease. *Please.*"

Mason didn't wait for her to ask again. He took hold of her wide hips and slid into her waiting warmth, sliding inch after inch into her silken sheath. She rippled around him, her body calling on his release even before he'd filled her completely.

Then he moved. Moved and wondered how the hell he'd ever touched another woman. This... With Lucy... Fuck, he didn't have the words to describe the bliss of her touch. This was more than just sex. This was... She was so wet, so tight, so hot and delicious. He fought against his release, clung to his sanity by a thread. He'd damned near come on his first thrust and he wasn't ready. He wanted her to linger on the cusp with him.

Mason slid out of her and then thrust forward once more, slamming their hips together and shaking the bed. It banged against the wall, a counterpoint to his thrusts. He repeated the motion—retreat and then slam home again. With every thrust her pussy clenched, milking his length as he filled her. Filled her over and over.

Their hips met over and again, the slapping of their flesh the only other sound to accompany their panting breath. That and his sweet Lucy's pleas.

"Mason," she panted. "Mason."

"Lucy," he murmured in return. Repeating her name was the one thing that kept him from getting utterly lost in her. "Lucy." He pounded her core. "Lucy." He picked up the pace. "Lucy." Sweat dripped down his spine.

Pleasure sang through his veins, coasting along his nerves and setting each one alight. The ecstasy snatched away all hints of control he might have had once upon a time. But being inside Lucy, claiming her body, destroyed any hint of what remained.

Back and forth, he thrust into her, fighting himself as he tried to decide whether to close his eyes and savor the sweet pulsing of her pussy as he fucked her. Or he could keep them open and watch as her expression revealed how much she needed him.

She wrapped her legs around him, pulling him inexplicably closer, and he groaned, pushing and pulling as she rolled her hips with him. Her walls squeezed his cock, and he thrust into her harder still, desperate to make them both quake and shudder with release.

"Yes," she gasped. "Perfect. *Need.*"

"*Yes,*" he hissed in response. He was everything she needed. He'd make sure of it.

"I'm gonna…" Lucy released the headboard and scrambled to snatch the sheets, claws digging into the fabric and tearing the cloth. She bucked into him harder and deeper than before as her pussy quaked and surged around his dick.

"That's it, baby." He didn't let his pace falter. "Come for me. Come on my cock and let me feel you."

And she did. A long, slow moan escaped her mouth, back arched, and lips parted as her body trembled and shook. His balls were tight against his body, the ache to let go nearly overwhelming him, but he held on. Just a little longer. Just a little…

Lucy screamed his name, mouth wide, and he watched in awe as her fangs slipped past her gums. "Let me, let me…"

He knew what she craved because he craved the same.

Mason bent low, fucking her through her orgasm, wringing every last bit of pleasure out of his mate until… Those pearly white fangs sank into his shoulder. She pierced his skin, adding pain to the pleasure that consumed him. She growled with her mouth touching his bleeding flesh, teeth sinking in deeper as if she wanted to be sure the scar took.

And that was too much for him to resist. Too much for him to hold out against. That deep pain triggered the ultimate pleasure, his body overtaken by ecstasy as he emptied himself inside her pussy. He jerked once, then twice, and slammed home a third time. His hips remained pressed tightly against hers as his cock twitched deep inside her. He allowed his fangs to burst past his gums, his wolf roaring to the forefront of his mind while pleasure still overcame him.

Mason bared his canines and didn't hesitate to claim his mate. His one. His savior.

His Lucy.

CHAPTER TWENTY-ONE

"AND THIS ONE'S FOR MY BIG BROTHER," KADE SHOUTED into the mic as he set the needle on a record.

Frank Sinatra's *Love and Marriage* blared from the sound system and the crowd cheered. Just about every member of the Blackwood pack had crammed into the pack house's living room-turned-reception hall to celebrate the mating of Mason and Lucy. It had been a long time coming, and they'd all known what had been at stake. Consequently, Lucy had been treated like their savior— which wasn't too far off, as far as Mason was concerned.

As the crowd sang along with the catchy tune and silly lyrics, Mason pushed his way past the bodies, his co-best man Gavin in tow. He stepped out onto the big front porch and took a deep lungful of fresh, crisp air. The music was just as loud outside, thanks to the portable speakers someone had set up.

"It's getting a little stuffy in there," Gavin said, leaning back against a porch rail.

"It's not much better out here," Mason observed.

Dozens more ceremony guests milled around outside, obviously as in need of a little elbow room as Mason. Most of the adults had champagne flutes in their hands and everyone was celebrating. And why not? Their alpha, who'd been dangerously close to losing his mind—which would have been bad for everyone—had just cemented the stability of their pack. If ever there was a day for a party, this was it.

The Tiptons spotted him from across the lawn and raised their glasses to him before Robert pulled Bonnie into his arms and started dancing with her. Lucy already had Charlie in her arms and was swinging him around and dipping him almost all the way to the ground. The kid giggled like it was the most fun he'd ever had in his life.

Kade joined his brothers, settling on the other side of Mason. Observing him. Especially the way all of his attention was focused on Lucy.

"It's like he's not even the same person," he grumbled toward Gavin.

"Good," Gavin replied. "I think Lucy is a good influence on him. I still can't believe she killed Frank with a fucking garden tool. She's one seriously bad-ass bitch."

Gavin stopped short, his eyes growing wide. Kade

grimaced. No doubt they were expecting Mason to react as he would have before he'd discovered his mate. Nearly feral Mason. But that Mason no longer existed. His brother was right—Lucy had a very calming effect on him, and he was no longer sent into an apoplectic rage over stupid shit. Only big shit mattered now.

"You're right about that," he said with a chuckle. "And she's all mine."

Movement caught his eye just in time to see Drew round the corner of the building. The Blackwood brothers followed.

"Hiding?" Mason asked as they caught up with the healer.

Drew smirked. "Congratulations, Mason."

Mason gripped the man's hand and grinned. "Thanks, even though you're probably pissed I didn't go feral. Bet you were counting the days till you could put me down."

Drew frowned. "No… I never… What makes you think…"

Mason let the poor guy sputter for a few seconds and then slapped him on the back. "It's okay, man. I wouldn't blame you, after the all the shit I gave you whenever you came close to Lucy."

"I'm not the kind of guy to hold a grudge," he said with a shrug and a smile.

"Glad to hear it. Now let's get back to the party."

They headed back and found Agnes Dickey holding onto

frail, little Arthur as they climbed the porch stairs. Mason and his brothers helped them both up and settled them onto the porch swing.

"Oh, goodness," Agnes laughed, completely out of breath. "Let me tell you something, boys, getting old isn't for the faint of heart."

"I'm surprised to see you two," Mason said, leaning back against the porch rail. "Thought you'd be at the diner."

"And miss the mating celebration?" Agnes asked, shocked as only little old Southern ladies could get. "I never thought this day would come, let me tell you. But you've found yourself a keeper, Mason."

"Thank you, Agnes."

She breathed a heavy sigh and shook her head, topped with a hair-sprayed helmet of grey. "You're such a nice boy. I would have been devastated if you'd gone feral, like that Riverson woman. Would have been a shame to put you down. Take my word for it, breaking in a new Ruling Circle is a royal pain in the ass."

Silence fell over the little group, and then Mason burst out laughing so hard he doubled over. It took a good minute for him to catch his breath again.

"Glad to know my life means so much to you, Agnes."

She shrugged. "Oh, it does, honey. Just sayin'."

Arthur nudged his wife. "Stop while you're ahead, my dear."

Mason glanced over at Lucy again, now playing with a group of little kids from the lessons she was taking in how to control her wolf. They all clearly adored her. Smart kids. She wore a white dress that hugged her curves better than that one Marilyn Monroe wore. She was a vision.

Warmth spread through his chest and then all through his body. He'd do anything for her, without hesitation, and for the rest of his life. He'd bedded plenty of women in his life, but even the most passionate affair paled in comparison to his love for Lucy. He'd changed so much since meeting her, and his capacity for love startled him.

As Lucy bent down to listen to whatever Charlie was prattling on about, Mason imagined the pup was theirs. He needed Lucy on a cellular level, but just past that was a need to see her belly heavy with his baby. He couldn't wait to hear its little squeals and yelps, to hold the squirming, shifting creature in his hands.

"Hey, Kade," he said, beckoning his brother over while his eyes never wavered from his mate.

"What's up, bro?"

"First thing in the morning, I need to you to head up to Pepper and pack up all of Lucy's belongings. Her grandmother too, if she'll let you."

"Sure thing, but I thought you two were going to make a road trip out of that."

A smile played on Mason's lips. "Change of plans. Lucy's not leaving pack lands until she's pregnant."

At that moment, Lucy glanced his way and smiled, and his heart lit up like a thousand suns.

LUCY'S HEART SWELLED UNTIL SHE THOUGHT IT WOULD burst. The intensity of her love for Mason made her want to laugh and cry and scream, all at the same time. Those feelings flooded her every time she looked at him, and every time she looked at him, she wanted to throw herself at him. And she had.

Since moving into the pack house the day after her parents' house had burned down, she'd barely let him leave their bedroom. Or rather, their bed.

He didn't seem to mind.

She was still feeling her way around her new role as alpha mate, but she'd embraced it wholeheartedly, determined to be the best damned alpha mate she could be. And that included paying attention to the pack's pups, like Charlie. Who was chattering away at her a mile a minute.

"...so there!" He gave her a satisfied smirk, but she had no clue why.

"I'm sorry, sweetie, what?"

He sighed dramatically at having to repeat himself. "I *said*...I shift faster than you, so there."

Right, they'd been teasing each other about their capabilities as shifters. *This is so surreal*, she thought. A week before, she'd been a normal girl, living a normal life. Now...

"I can't deny that but tell you something." She leaned in close and arched an eyebrow at him. "Who's better at *controlling* their shifts?"

"Doesn't matter," Charlie shot back.

"Does so."

"Does not!" He stuck his tongue out playfully.

"Fine," she said. "You're a better shifter. But Ghosty likes me better."

It was a low blow and she knew it.

"Nuh uh!" Charlie was outraged by the mere suggestion.

"Uh huh!"

He shook his head frantically. "No she doesn't. She loves me best, and I'm going to name *all* the kittens so they like me best too, so there!"

"I want to name a kitten too," whined a little girl, running up to join them. Soon a half dozen other pups ran up, all demanding to be part of the naming process.

"Tell you what," Lucy said loudly, demanding their attention without having to resort to shouts or snarls. As soon as they'd quieted and were all staring up at her, she continued. "Tell you what. Why don't you all go inside and suggest some names? You can all vote on each name, and the ones with the most votes win."

The kids shot each other glances and then tore off toward the house, each trying to reach the kittens before the rest. Lucy smiled after them, eager to have her own pup join their ranks. She was jolted out of her reverie by a light tap on her shoulder.

Spinning around, she found a lovely older woman in a gauzy purple dress. She had an aura of serenity about her and Lucy liked her immediately.

"I'm Ida Abbot," the woman said, shaking Lucy's hand gently. "I manage the pack house. I'm sorry I haven't introduced myself before now, but things have been a little… hectic."

Lucy laughed. "You can say that again."

"I just wanted to tell you how happy we all are that Mason finally found his mate and that you've joined our wonderful little family."

"Not as happy as I am. Before I met Mason, I was wandering around rudderless. I only had my grandmother and my best friend to keep me on course." She let her grateful gaze skim over the knots of people gathered to celebrate her mating with their alpha. "Now I feel like I'm part of a real family again. I don't think I have the words to express how fulfilling that is."

Ida reached out and laid a cool, dry hand on Lucy's. "I can imagine, after all the trauma you've suffered."

Lucy blinked in surprise. "Word sure does travel fast in the Blackwood pack."

"Can't deny that," Ida said with a soft chuckle. "Word also got around that you killed an alpha with a… garden hoe. Is that really true?"

A few people had broached the subject with her before, but she didn't like talking about that night. She'd only discussed it with Mason a couple of times, and Drew once, when he'd examined her for injuries. But Ida had a way about her that crumbled Lucy's self-defenses. She knew she could trust this woman with her deepest secrets.

"People talk about it like I did something amazing," she started, her voice catching in her throat from the emotions dredged up by the memory. "All I can really say is that knowing I took a life certainly doesn't feel amazing. Don't get me wrong, I'd do it again without hesitation. He was trying to kill Mason and me. I had no other choice but to protect my mate."

"It probably didn't help that all those years ago he'd stood by while his mate murdered your parents."

Lucy shook her head, swallowing the grief trying to bubble up inside her. It was a happy day. The happiest of her life and she wouldn't spoil it by dredging up that ugliness.

She sensed Mason approaching long before Ida glanced over Lucy's shoulder at him. She also sensed his amusement over something.

"The pups are inside shouting kitten names at each other so loudly that no one can hear Sinatra anymore. Don't suppose you had anything to do with that, my love?"

Lucy grinned up at him and wrapped an arm around his waist. "I plead the fifth. But I can go settle them down—"

"No," he said, pulling her tight into his side. "You spend enough time with them already."

"I just can't wait to have one of our own," she sighed wistfully.

Ida's gaze bounced between them for a moment, and then she grasped their free hands and smiled. "Don't fret. The pups will come much sooner than you expect. For now, enjoy the time you have together."

Lucy dropped her head back to gaze up at the man she loved, the man she knew deep in her gut she could never live without. The father of her future children, the alpha of the pack, the keeper of her heart.

"I think I can manage that."

IF YOU ENJOYED THIS BOOK, PLEASE BE TOTALLY awesomesauce and leave a review so others may discover it as well. Long review or short, your opinion will help other readers make future purchasing decisions. So, go forth and rate our level-o-awesome!

REAL MEN SHIFT ISN'T THE ONLY SERIES IN THE REAL MEN Universe. We've also got Real Men of Othercross— some very sexy vamps that can't wait to have a nibble of their mates.

Check out Book 1, Vampire Seduction now!

Alena Falkov speed-walked through the halls of Othercross Vampire Judiciary in a pathetic attempt at punctuality. After a hundred and twenty-one years of perpetual tardiness, she should have given up any pretense of having her shit in order, but hope sprang eternal.

Good thing, since she was an eternal being.

The memory of waking up covered in blood next to a completely hungover cowboy flashed in her mind. Just her luck to have been changed by some drunk loser of a vampire instead of a gorgeous billionaire master who whisked her away to some exotic locale where he showered her with everything her heart desired.

Not that jets had been invented back then. The point was

that a girl still had to work for a living, even if she was undead. And working meant *not* being late to her job because even if she didn't have a grocery bill, rent was still due in cold, hard cash every damn month. And for some weird reason landlords didn't have much of a sense of humor about late payments.

Go figure.

If only vamp life was as sparkly and romantic as it was in the movies. Hell, she'd settle for a story arc in a romance novel right about now. The down-on-her-luck vampiress about to be evicted from her shithole apartment meets a hot-blooded master yearning for her—his fated mate, his one true love, his beloved—to join him in bringing down the evil genius plotting to take over the world.

Alena was jostled out of her pretty daydream when she bumped into a harried werewolf paralegal—Charlotte something, if memory served—who growled menacingly as she struggled to hold onto the stack of files in her arms. Alena did her best not to smirk at the she-wolf's bravado and then muttered an apology and let the woman get on with her busy evening. Hers too, for that matter.

"Late again, Falkov?" an amused voice said from behind her and Alena winced.

She was *always* late after Professor Heidgerken's Comparative Constitutional Law in Shifter Societies class at Othercross University. The warlock really loved the sound of his own voice, a fact which didn't seem to impress her boss, Odofin, all that much.

Alena jabbed the elevator's up button and then turned a glare on the owner of the voice. "I'm not late, Ryan. I'm *fashionable*."

Ryan's lips curled into a smirk. "Is unemployment fashionable these days? I'd try that look, but I don't really think homeless shelter chic is my thing."

Alena crossed her arms and gave Ryan's lean frame a dubious once-over. "Says the fairy wearing a buttercup yellow cardigan and green plaid slacks."

One dark eyebrow shot up and he fluttered his wings, just to tease her. "Drinks tonight?"

The elevator doors opened and Alena hurried on. "Only if you're paying."

"Admit it," he called as the doors cut him off from view, "I make this outfit look *good*."

As much as she wanted to stay and argue fashion with her friend, he was right. Unemployment wasn't her color even if yellow and plaid were his. The moment the doors cracked open, Alena rushed out and nearly tripped over the stench that hit her like a sledgehammer.

"Where are you hiding, Owens?" She looked around for the owner of the scent she knew almost as well as her own. "Don't bother. I can smell you a mile away."

An Othercross enforcement officer turned the nearest corner, dragging a cowboy in handcuffs toward the elevator bank. A veritable Vampire Judiciary regular. If Owens wasn't brought in on drunk and disorderly charges at least once a month, she started to worry. Not much, but she couldn't ignore the tiny soft spot in her heart for the vampire who transformed her from a basic human to a just-as-basic immortal.

"Aw, shucks, darlin'," Owens slurred as he stumbled closer, his beat-up shitkickers scuffing the pristine hallway floors. "Man's got to enjoy hisself."

"Problem is, you aren't a man."

He leered at her good-naturedly. "Gimme jus' one night, I'll prove you wrong. Shtill have wha' it takes, shister."

She patted his scruffy cheek as the officer hustled him onto the elevator she'd just exited. "You had your shot, stud, and we know how *that* turned out. Lay off the sorority girls, m'kay? You know drinking from inebriated humans makes you tipsy too. One day you'll get yourself into real trouble instead of just a night in the drunk tank."

"Ah, 'Lena," he mewled as the doors closed on his ripe odor, no doubt headed for the vampire cell blocks in the basement so he could sleep it off.

Two minutes wasted! On Owens, of all people. She would have much rather spent the time debating the merits of secondhand clothes with Ryan. Not that she had the time to do that, either.

Picking up her pace, Alena's heels clicked loudly on the polished marble floors. As a vampire, she normally didn't make noise when she walked, but she'd found shifters could be notoriously jumpy when a vampire approached them without making a sound, especially from behind. It was a simple courtesy that cost her little and gained the appreciation of her coworkers.

Relief swelled in her chest when she caught sight of the Others Defense Office, but just as she reached for the door, a hand grabbed her from behind. Her fangs pulsed for a half-second before she swallowed her instinctive reaction.

It was Ebrey Carlson, a Vampire Judiciary paralegal. Her brown eyes snapped, flickers of yellow fire bursting in her irises. She tucked a dark curl behind one ear, shifting from one foot to the other several times, clearly upset about something.

"Alena, what moron thought it would be a good idea to give Devon Sinclair a case for judgment in front of a Triune for a vampire?"

Alena gaped. "What!"

See, this was the crap that happened when she was late.

"That's what *I* said," Ebrey huffed, throwing her hands in the air. "There has to be a mistake. Sinclair's a *wolf*, for blood's sake, and he hasn't even passed the bar yet. The client will never see daylight again, guilty or not, with that puppy repping him. Was someone asleep when the assignments were handed out?"

"Well, I certainly didn't assign him any cases, so it must have been Odofin," Alena replied grimly. "I can't imagine why. Hell, I'd do a better job than Devon, and I'm just Odofin's assistant."

Ebrey frowned. "Girl, don't get down on yourself. You have more experience than most of the actual lawyers here, even if you're still a law student. That poor sap would be a thousand times better off with you than Devon. I mean, come on, he couldn't even get into OC Law School. He went through the *human* education system."

Warmth from borrowed blood flooded Alena's cheeks at the compliment. It wasn't really in her nature to toot her own horn, so she relied on supportive friends and colleagues to remind her that she wasn't a total loser—even if she felt like one most of the time.

"Guess I'd better ask Odofin about it," she sighed and turned toward the door once again, but Ebrey stopped her again.

"Not if you want the defendant to have a fighting chance. The Triune's already been convened."

"Are you shitting me? How did this happen? I checked the schedule this morning before I left and Devon wasn't even slated to *assist* anyone, let alone open for a case."

Ebrey gave her a helpless shrug.

"By the blood, if Devon screws this up…" Alena glanced at the door one more time and then turned on her heel and headed back toward the elevators.

"Wait, are you going up there?" Ebrey asked, eyes wide with surprise while she hurried to keep up.

"Of course, I am. I didn't join the Others Defense Office for the fame and fortune, my friend. I want to make sure everyone who needs a defense lawyer gets one. A *good* one. Not some wolf shifter with a store-bought degree from a no-name human school. Everyone knows Harbor Law School hands out degrees to whoever has a fat checkbook."

"Harvard," Ebrey corrected.

Alena flapped an unconcerned hand. "Whatever. They got nothing on Othercross University."

Coincidentally, *Alena's* university.

"Won't Odofin be pissed that you're interfering with his assignments? Not to mention being hella late for work?"

Alena mentally remapped her entire evening as they rushed back to the elevators, not bothering with clicking her heels this time. First, she'd do what she could to help the defendant and then she'd deal with her boss. He couldn't yell at her for being late if she was off cleaning up his mess.

"Right now, I don't really care." She jabbed the up button. "I'll happily face his wrath once I'm sure Devon's not going to screw the client sideways with his ineptitude."

"Dude, it was nice working with you."

Alena scowled at her friend. "Thanks a lot," she drawled.

The doors opened and released a gaggle of vampires. Alena scurried on and realized she had no idea where she was going.

"Which courtroom?" she raised her voice over the crowd so Ebrey could hear her.

"Eight. Do you need my help?"

"No, I'll handle this. I'll get in, request a recess and a reassignment of counsel, and get out with my hand wrapped around Devon's furry neck. He should know better."

Ebrey saluted Alena as the doors closed, leaving her to her thoughts—primarily centered around what the hell Odofin had been thinking. After being his assistant for the last twenty years or so, she'd earned his trust in assigning the cases they received. Sure, he still dabbled in them occasionally, but he mostly left it to Alena to handle. He had better things to do, such as sucking up to high-ranking politicians. Alena couldn't remember a time when he'd messed up so royally though.

The doors opened on the crowded eighth floor. She barely managed an insincere apology as she pushed through a group of people standing in the middle of the hall like they owned the area. She almost knocked a stack of files out of the arms of the same wild-eyed, wild-haired paralegal as earlier. *Oops.*

Dammit, who used paper these days, anyway? Everything should be digitized by now. But *nooo*, the uppers were still stuck in the '80s—maybe the 1880s—not quite realizing a few decades had passed and computers were officially A Thing now.

Ironic that she wished for the mystery client's hardcopy case file as she rushed toward Courtroom Eight, trying not to sweat blood-tinged stains on her blouse. Good thing it was already red.

Alena stopped in her tracks and took a deep, calming breath. No matter how crazy the situation, the Triune wouldn't look kindly on her bursting into the courtroom in a fit of pique. Calm. Professional. Courteous. Not cra—

The scent registered a split second later, taking with it all thoughts of calm and professional.

Dizziness washed over her in an awful moment of disorientation—one when she could have been a snack for any passing predator. She'd been drunk before. She'd been high. She'd lost herself to the throes of passion, both during sex and during bloodlust as she drank down the rich, hot nectar of a willing donor. All of it—and none of it—described the fire that rushed through her veins.

Alena doubled over, hands on her knees, panting heavily,

and then forced herself to straighten as her head cleared. It all happened in the space of a few seconds, even though it felt like an eternity.

Dark chocolate, peppercorns, and the aroma of a gently burning fire imprinted on her soul—smoky and spicy with the hint of bitter sweetness. Every instinct demanded she find the owner of the scent. Abandon all tasks and responsibilities and claim what—*who*—belonged to her.

She'd never experienced anything like it, but Alena knew instinctively what it was, beyond any doubt. The connection to her beloved, the one chance she would have in her immortal life to find a true mate.

Alena hesitated for another moment, torn between following what every cell in her body screamed for her to do, and duty. The scent was strong and unfading, which suggested her beloved wasn't moving away from her. Or toward her. In fact, he wasn't moving at all.

Eyes narrowed, she propelled herself forward, realizing the scent intensified with each step she took closer to Courtroom Eight. She stared at the ornately carved wooden doors, certainty heavy in her gut. Her beloved was inside, among those attending the trial. A witness? A reporter? A family member of the accused, or maybe even the victim?

The possibilities, and each of their inevitable complications, ran through her mind as she heaved open one of the massive doors. Well, nothing worth having was ever easy. If her beloved was connected to the defendant or the victim, she would recuse herself from any work on the case. *After* ensuring a competent attorney had taken Devon's place.

Slipping just inside the doors, she scanned the handful of people in the courtroom. The Triune judges—all of whom she recognized—filed onto the dais in their regal purple robes as Devon Sinclair spoke with his client.

On the prosecution's side sat one of Alena's relatives she didn't really know, other than by reputation. Malone Falkov, her second cousin twice removed, if she had her vampiric family tree correct. As humans, they didn't share a drop of the same blood, but as vampires, they were somehow connected. Distantly, thank goodness. He was a shark of a prosecutor.

Behind Malone sat his immediate superior, Gretchen Bubák—no doubt sent to babysit Alena's relative. Malone had a earned a reputation as a hothead, and she'd heard he was on the verge of being sacked from OCVJ—Othercross Vampire Judiciary. Strange that he'd be prosecuting *any* case. Maybe it was his last chance to prove himself.

She recognized every guard and the handful of people sitting watching the proceedings from the cheap seats. The only person she didn't know was the man sitting at Devon Sinclair's side—in the chair reserved for the accused. Alena's brain churned quickly to find any reason —other than the most obvious—that a person would sit in that particular chair.

There was none. And the scent trail led directly to him.

The defendant was her beloved.

Fucking figured.

See, this was the crap that happened when she was late.

Check out Book 1, Vampire Seduction now!

ABOUT THE AUTHORS

CELIA KYLE

Ex-dance teacher, former accountant and erstwhile collectible doll salesperson, New York Times and USA Today bestselling author Celia Kyle now writes paranormal romances. It goes without saying that there's always a happily-ever-after for her characters, even if there are a few road bumps along the way. Today she lives in central Florida and writes full-time with the support of her loving husband and two finicky cats.

Website

Facebook

MARINA MADDIX

New York Times & USA Today Bestselling Author Marina Maddix is a romantic at heart, but hates closing the bedroom door on her readers. Her stories are sweet, with just enough spice to make your mother blush. She lives with her husband and cat near the Pacific Ocean, and loves to hear from her fans.

Website

Facebook

Printed in Great Britain
by Amazon